obsessive CRAVINGS

obsessive CRAVINGS

WICKED CRAVINGS

BOOK ONE

JL JACKOLA

Paperback ISBN 978-1-960784-39-1
Hardback ISBN 978-1-960784-40-7
Electronic ISBN 978-1-960784-38-4
Library of Congress Control Number: 2024908632

Distributed by Tivshe Publishing
Printed in the United States of America

Cover design by Dark Queen Designs

Visit www.jljackola.com

Also by J. L. Jackola

UNBOUND PROPHECY SERIES

Ascension

Descent

Surfacing

Submerged

Riven

Adrift

UNBOUND PROPHECY NOVELS

Unbound Kingdom (the trilogy omnibus)

Orlaina (an Unbound Prophecy prequel)

UNBOUND KINGDOM TRILOGY

Severed Kingdom

Cursed Kingdom

Prophesied Kingdom

HUES SERIES

The Forgotten Hues of Skye

The Coveted Hues of Skye

The Shattered Shades of Crimson

The Impossible Shades of Crimson

The Endless Shadows of Pete

Author's Note

Welcome to the world of wicked cravings where morally gray is the norm and cravings are hard to resist.

Obsessive Cravings is a dark romance with a mafia theme so be prepared to expect:

Explicit sexual content
Language
Threats of s. a. (not by the mmc)
Stalking (definitely by the mmc)
Past trauma
Violence and death

For those who crave the morally gray bad boy.

Chapter One

There were few things I didn't get when I wanted them. And Riley Brinks was one thing I wanted. One thing I was planning to make mine. A pretty little thing who was moving to my city, willingly walking into my game so I could play with her.

Riley was exactly why I never acted swiftly to take down my enemies. Patience offered the chance for them to become complacent, to think I'd forgotten their mistakes. And it offered me the opportunity to enact the most ruthless payback possible. Mason Brinks was Riley's older brother and since Mason was on my list of enemies, Riley's sudden move to my city meant my patience had paid off.

When I'd seen her application on the desk of an associate, I hadn't given it much thought, but her name had stuck in my mind. That name had hounded me until I discovered the reason. Brinks was a name I knew well. Mason Brinks was a ruthless bastard who owned the western part of the province. He had his hands in every business from the city to the farms of Treemont, where he lived. He and I had been rivals for years since the moment he tried stepping into my city. No one threatened my rule on Bridgeville. This city was mine.

I'd run his attempts out and we'd been enemies since. I'd spent years sitting silently, waiting for just the right moment to strike back, to enact a revenge he wouldn't see coming. A revenge that would leave him so wounded he'd never recover, and his territory would become mine. My patience with Mason's arrogance had now presented me with Riley, who was the crown jewel of rewards.

Her choice of cities intrigued me. It made no sense for someone inside Mason's inner circle to move to enemy territory. I wasn't sure if he was sending her here to infiltrate my business or if she was a rogue player. Either way, I'd initially intended to shut her down and give her no ability to move to Bridgeville. But when I'd seen a picture of the beauty, I knew she had to be mine. My plan had formulated instantly and whether she was coming to hunt me or not, she had now become my prey. I wanted a taste of Riley Brinks before I ruined her completely and used her to bring her brother down.

I looked out over the view from my office, knowing she was down there, moving her things in and preparing for a new life in my world. She wouldn't see me coming, but I'd make sure she would never look away once she did.

Tempting her had been easy enough. Running a city had its advantages, and I ensured my people made her an offer she couldn't resist. I owned most of the businesses in town, including the brokerage firm that outbid my associate's tiny advisor office. He couldn't complain—I only let him run that office because he'd done me a favor once.

Once she accepted, I ensured an apartment was available in a building I owned, one close enough for me to observe her and take the first steps in my plan to manipulate her.

Running my hands through my hair, I grabbed the picture from my folder on her, staring at her, memorizing every detail, my craving for her already festering. She'd stepped into my web, and I was going to tangle her in so deep, her brother would never get her out. My only worry was that I would get tangled in it as well. I'd never been this obsessed with a woman. She was eighteen years younger than me, a mere twenty-seven years old, but I didn't care. I would have Riley Brinks. She was mine, even if she didn't know it yet. And when I had my fill of her, I would leave her ruined and finally destroy her brother.

Chapter Two

RILEY

Running.

That's what I was doing.

Running from reality. Running from lies. Running from fear.

And where was I after days of running? In a city I didn't know, starting a new life, and standing in a tiny studio apartment, listening as the movers thumped down the stairs. I wanted to run again because this was a disaster. Furniture cluttered every inch of space, and I didn't know where to begin.

"Damn," I muttered, trying to close the door, which was wedged behind my sofa. I blew a strand of hair from my eyes and shoved the sofa a few times to gain some leverage on the door. Flopping onto the couch, I cursed myself for not researching better when I'd left Treemont.

Ran from Treemont was more like it. I'd been planning my escape for months. After finally getting all my plans in place, I had left without a word, without a single glance back, because looking back would have been a costly mistake. I knew what was in that rearview mirror, and it held nothing but terror.

I'd left it all behind, and I didn't want to look back, no matter how much it hurt me.

"Wow, that is a lot of furniture."

I peered up to see a tall blonde about my age with large brown eyes and an amethyst stud in her petite nose. She had her hair piled in messy curls, giving her the appearance that she'd just rolled out of bed. It was cute, and I had a moment of hair envy because my heavy hair only rebelled against styles like that.

"Did you neglect to look at the pictures before you moved in?"

"No, I saw them," I admitted with a sigh. "I think I just convinced myself the pictures made it look smaller than it would be."

She shook her head and laughed. "Naïve and delusional. You should fit right in."

"Oh good. I was worried those traits would make me stand out," I said, rising from the couch.

"I'm Ava," she said. "My apartment is just down the hall."

I gave the couch another shove. "Riley and I now live here and possibly in the hall if I don't figure out how to get this couch to shrink."

"Here, let me help. I've been dealing with these studios for a few years. You learn some tricks." She glanced around at my mess. "Although, I'd recommend paring down."

"Definitely on my to do list."

With Ava's help, the couch moved enough to free the door.

"I'd offer you a drink but, even if I could get to my fridge, there's nothing in it yet," I said, as Ava leaned on the doorframe.

"Nah, I'm on my way to work. Maybe once you get unpacked. If you need anything, just knock. I work nights at the bar around the corner, but I'm usually around most days."

"Thanks. And thanks for the help with the couch."

Saying goodbye to Ava, I shut the door and stared at the mess. I was starting my new job in the morning, and I didn't even know where my clothes were. It was overwhelming, and I had a nagging feeling that I'd made the wrong decision. That running was something I shouldn't have done. That I should have faced the lies instead of fleeing.

"Too late now, Riley."

After placing a few items for sale on the local marketplace, I maneuvered what furniture I could and unpacked what I needed for the next day. Too tired to even order dinner, I flopped into the corner I'd cleared on my bed. Thoughts of my past and of home cascaded through my mind and a melancholy crept in before I pushed it aside. The morning would be a start to my new life, a new adventure, and I held onto that thought as my weariness overcame me.

MY PHONE ALARM jerked me awake, and I sat up quickly, startled by my unfamiliar surroundings. After struggling to find my phone in the tangle of clothes piled around me, I quickly dressed and ran out the door, realizing I hadn't taken time to figure out how far the office was from my apartment. In fact, I wasn't even sure where that office was.

I'd interviewed at a firm on the upper east end of the city, finding an apartment online that stated it was within walking distance. But I'd never been to the office, having taken all my interviews by phone or virtual meetings. Treemont was a two-day ride from Bridgeville and since the company was eager to have me, they had obliged to long distance interviews. It still seemed strange that they'd reached out to me. I had been job hunting, thinking Bridgeville was far enough away and offered me the opportunity to blend in. It was a metropolis compared to tiny Treemont. But I hadn't considered this firm, thinking the smaller one would be a better place to start as I adjusted to city life.

As I was looking down at the map on my phone, trying to determine where the closest coffee shop was, something yanked my purse from my arm. I looked up, seeing my purse in the hands of a lanky teenager who winked at me and ran.

I opened my mouth to yell when a man stepped around me and grabbed the boy, stopping his getaway with a quick jerk of his large hand.

"I don't think this belongs to you," he said, snatching my purse back as the boy stumbled backward, eyes wide before he ran off.

That expression 'deer in headlights' was one I always thought was cliché, but that's exactly how I felt, and when the owner of that deep baritone turned his navy eyes to me, I remained frozen. He was tall and built from what I could see from the fit of his expensive coat. His thick brown hair had flecks of gray just around the temples, giving a mature addition to his rugged features. My jaw was dropping when I stopped it, composing myself as he handed my purse back.

"A little advice from someone who has spent his entire life here. Don't stand out like a tourist when you walk the streets," he said, his baritone gripping my insides.

"Thank you," I said, trying not to stutter like a teenager. "Is it that obvious?"

He smiled, something that only made him more handsome. "Definitely."

I glanced down at my phone, kicking myself for my bashful reaction to his smile. Looking back up, I said, "Thank you again."

He gave me a nod and turned.

"Do you know where I can find a coffee shop?" I asked, desperate to have this man in my company for a few more minutes but not understanding why.

He turned back to me, giving me a boyish grin. "You *are* new, aren't you?"

"Very. Last night was my first night."

His eyes studied me, making me feel very seen. "Which way are you headed?"

"Upper east side," I said. "22nd Street."

"Come on. You need to go off the beaten path to find the best shops. If you go to the ones on the main streets, you'll get the tourist coffee. It's like water with a hint of coffee."

Smiling, I thanked him again. He made idle chatter until he led me to a small coffee shop two blocks from where I needed to be. There was a strange restraint to him. Not that I knew him, but his conversation seemed restrained, kept to the basics of the city and landmarks. When he left me at the shop, I realized I hadn't even gotten his name and wished I had, no matter that I didn't need to involve anyone in my life right now. It was risky...but I'd been lonely for a long time, and I liked having someone come to my rescue like he had.

"There are no knights in shining armor, Riley," I scolded myself. There were only men who turned on you.

I ordered my coffee and made my way to the firm. Standing before the high rise, I looked around. This couldn't be it. This was a massive building. I walked around the corner, seeing the firm name on the outside, the offices within. The advisory firm I'd worked for in Treemont had been in a refurbished house. It was small with a hometown feel. Nothing about this firm said hometown, and nerves abounded in me.

New life. New experiences, I told myself.

This was what I'd signed up for. There was no turning back now. I returned to the front of the building and made my way in, trying not to look like the newbie that I felt like. The lobby was enormous. A guard station sat in the middle, elevators to their left, and to their right was a hallway that led to what looked like a private elevator.

"Riley Brinks?" I turned to the sound of my name, seeing a face that seemed familiar.

"Ken Stevens," he said, extending his hand. This was my new

manager. I recognized him from the virtual interviews. He was tall with thick graying hair and glasses that framed his green eyes.

"Ken. Hi, it's so nice to meet you. This place is huge!"

"We are the largest firm in the city, and we have the best spot. It helps when your owner also owns most of the real estate in town."

"Greyson Tides also owns the building?" I said. Ken had dropped the name enough during our interviews to know Greyson Tides was the most powerful businessman in Bridgeville. Something about that intrigued me. The way Ken spoke his name was beyond respect, as if there was power in it. And a man whose name alone held power made me curious.

"That's right. Come on in, I'll show you around."

Ken led me into the open lobby of the firm, which took up most of the first floor. He chatted to me as he gave me the tour and introduced me to my new co-workers. After showing me to my office, which was three times the size of what I'd had at my old firm, he left me to get settled.

Gazing out the window, I had a strange sense of disbelief, as if I would wake up and find myself back in Treemont at any minute. Everything seemed surreal and so far out of my comfort zone that the instinct to flee and run back home hit me again. But returning home wasn't an option. I'd made my choice and now I was here. There was nothing more to do than to keep moving forward. Looking backward was too painful.

Chapter Three

GREYSON

"Good morning, Mr. Tides," my assistant, Sherry, said as I walked through the doors.

"That asshole, Turnkin's son, was stealing purses again. Call Den and have him pay them a visit."

"Yes, Mr. Tides."

I closed my office door, loosening my tie and pulling out my folder on Riley again. The picture of her didn't do her justice. She was breathtaking. Those green eyes had been pools of emerald, standing out against the ebony of her hair. Those lips had parted when I turned to her, and I hadn't been able to stop the thoughts of how I wanted to use them. They were full and a natural blush, the same blush her cheeks had grown as she'd dropped her eyes from me. The way her skirt had fit her curves and her black pumps had emphasized her calves left me imagining what was under that skirt.

While I hadn't intended for her to see me, instead wanting to follow her steps and watch her, the circumstance had been fortuitous. Offering me an opportunity to earn her trust and to get close to her. Although, now that I'd been that close, I wondered if being anywhere else would be as satisfying. The scent of her perfume still lingered in my mind along with the smile that had put warmth in my chest where only ice had been for far too long.

My initial thoughts that her brother had sent her to Bridgeville faded the moment I started watching her. There were no bodyguards with her—my men had scoured the building and the block for any sign. She'd driven to town by herself, her car now stored in one of my parking garages. I could find no evidence to support the theory that Mason was involved, which told me she was alone. A surprising revelation, considering my animosity toward her brother. That could only mean she'd come here to rebel, or he didn't know. The latter option made no sense, because Mason was too controlling to let that happen. Her presence was a mystery, but I'd take it as a gift that would only make my revenge sweeter.

Walking to the window of my penthouse office, I waited for her to round the corner, knowing exactly what direction she would come from. I'd given her the directions before I'd left her at the coffee shop, part of me wanting to linger, to continue hearing the sweet drawl of her accent and seeing the way the morning light sparkled in her eyes. Another part wondered at the effect she was having on me after just that brief interaction. It was dangerous, obsessive almost.

She came into sight, holding her cup of coffee in both hands as she looked around. I couldn't help but chuckle. Even from this high up, I could see the childlike wonder in her eyes. It was apparent that Mason had kept her sheltered. His territory held a city, not one as extensive as mine, but large enough for her to not be so overwhelmed by stepping into one. Sheltering her had been a mistake because now she was mine for the taking. Mine to use and mine to taste. I didn't like the way my body reacted to those thoughts. I'd envisioned how I'd use her, manipulating her into my bed and marking her as mine. Destroying her and returning her to Mason so he'd know that I'd been the one to mark her. But being in her presence had been intoxicating, and after seeing her, I wanted to do more. I wanted to own her, to ruin her for any other man. And I was no longer so certain I wanted to return her. The need to keep her pounded through me.

My phone chimed, and I looked down at it. I'd had my tech guy connect to Riley's phone and all her devices overnight.

"My, my little girl," I said, scrolling through the marketplace ad she'd placed to sell her furniture. I gritted my teeth, seeing that she'd put her phone number on the posting. Naïve to a fault. I wondered if her brother knew what keeping her in a protective shell had done. And if he knew she'd just walked into the lion's den. "You shouldn't be so revealing with your information, little girl. This town will devour you. And I'm the only one who gets to devour you."

AFTER TASKING Sherry with taking care of Riley's furniture ad, I had her call the firm manager, Ken, to my office.

My knuckles cracked as I patiently waited for him to arrive, my mind going through the first pieces of my plan to bring Riley to her knees. The thought put visions of what I'd do to her once she was there in my head. I was wrestling to calm my body down when Sherry buzzed to tell me Ken had arrived. Cursing my dirty mind, I told her to send him in.

"Greyson," he said, entering with the confidence of someone who had been in my network long enough to have the privilege of using my first name.

"Sit, Ken. Tell me about her," I said. He didn't have to ask why I was asking the question. I'd ensured he would treat Riley as if she were the most important asset to the firm...which she now was.

"She's something. I don't think I've ever seen such bright green eyes, and that hair—"

I slammed my fist on the desk, leaning forward. "Not her looks, Ken," I said, my teeth clenched. "Don't make me send your wife the number of the woman you meet for drinks every Tuesday after work."

His swallow was loud, and he sat up straighter in his seat. "No, you don't need to do that. I told you when I interviewed Riley—she's smart, focused, and professional. She'll do fine."

"You gave her the large window office?"

He fidgeted in his seat, looking even more uncomfortable. "Bill wasn't happy. I had to offer him a few extra vacation days to get him to comply. He was still grumbling about it until I told him the order came down from you."

"Let me know if he gives her a hard time. And if anyone in that office, employee or client, gives her trouble, I want to know about it immediately."

He nodded before he asked, "What's so special about her? I've never seen you take an interest in the firm or any of the staff there."

"That's my business and something you don't need to worry about. Just make sure she remains content or heads will roll and secrets will spill."

I had enough dirt on everyone in that office to fire them all. The only reason I even owned the firm was to keep the feds occupied. If they were snooping to find dirt on me, they'd hit all the legal businesses. The illegal ones I had buried so far below the red tape that layered my legal businesses, no one would ever discover them. Having been in the business as long as I had, most of the illegal ones were liquidated by now, the money reinvested in real estate or other entities where it was untraceable. But there were a few out there that were better left unseen.

"Understood," Ken said, waiting for further direction.

"Go back to the office. And buy her lunch today, but don't take her out," I added quickly, the idea of another male with her stirring my envy. "Just make sure we pick up the tab."

"Will do."

After he left my office, I sat back, contemplating why the thought of her with another man had been so uncomfortable. I shook it off as Sherry knocked and peeked her head in.

"I reached out and bought all the furniture. I have someone meeting her this week to pay her and pick it up."

"Perfect. Donate it to the thrift shop outside of the city. I don't want her finding it. But before you do, I want to look through it."

She gave me a curious glance but didn't comment. She knew better than to question me.

"Yes, sir," she replied, shutting the door and leaving me to my thoughts again. Those thoughts were of the gorgeous ebony haired beauty who was now one step closer to becoming mine.

Chapter Four

My first few days at work were dull, consisting of mundane tasks like training and setting up my office. The exciting part was exploring the city during my lunch breaks and after work. Bridgeville was massive compared to the small town of Treemont. Skyscrapers towered to the clouds, people bustled on every street, and cars beeped and idled at stoplights. But I'd discovered that a few blocks from the main part of the city, a transition began that led to regal homes, people walking their dogs, and children playing. The dichotomy was striking.

My studio apartment made me feel suffocated every time I returned to it. I missed the sprawling lawns of my brother's home, the horses in the fields, the farmers tending their crops. And I missed my brother, Mason. I'd been cold to him in the months I was planning my escape, knowing that escape was from him and the life of lies he'd built for me. Finding out his money hadn't come from the real estate business he owned, that he ran a mafia-like business, one that involved guns and violence and everything else my stunned mind didn't want to admit. I wanted to be as far from him as possible. I'd been blind, naïve, purposely fed lies to keep me safe. Or at least that's what he told me it was all for.

I'd always wondered why he kept me close, insisting I live nearby and stay in Treemont. I'd never questioned the men who walked the grounds of his large estate, ones he had insisted couldn't touch me...until one did.

"Shit," I grumbled as my key slipped, my finger jamming on the doorknob. I needed to focus. It had been a long day, and I'd grabbed some takeout on the way home. A few days before, someone had bought all my furniture, offering me so much for it I couldn't argue when she insisted on everything but my bed. It was enough for me to buy new furniture and more. A moving service had picked it up yesterday, handing me an envelope of cash, then driving away with what remained of my old life.

I was looking forward to spending the cash on a shopping trip now that the weekend was here, but for now, I just wanted to sit on my bed and eat the fries in my hand. Finally getting the key to cooperate, I threw open my door and gasped, my jaw dropping to the floor. The bare apartment was decorated as if the finest interior decorator had spent months perfecting it. A loveseat of plush green and a small round table with two chairs lined with that same green sat where the small kitchen was. There was a rug with hints of the same green in it, the design reminding me of the fields of wheat at home.

A thick fluffy gray comforter was on my bed, decorative pillows with white peonies and red petals scattered atop it. Even the walls now held pictures that were reminders of home, as if someone knew the intimate details of my likes and dislikes. A bookshelf lined the wall across from my bed, and my eyes took in the dark romance titles that currently filled my e-reader.

"Holy fuck," I mumbled, walking in and dropping my food on the mahogany table.

I wandered around the apartment, trying to understand how this had happened until fear gripped me. Had he found me? My heart raced, and I backed up, knocking into a chair and grasping the back of it to steady myself. I was trying not to hyperventilate, panic seizing me as my eyes looked around wildly, landing on a note propped against the new backsplash on my counter. With hesitation, I moved my feet and grabbed the note. My hands were shaking, my mind trying to work out how I could run again. Where I could go without a job, without preparation, like I'd had before. It had been so much work, knowing Mason tracked everything I did. He was even tracking my phone until I'd bought a new one without telling him, continuing to use the original one so he wouldn't know. It was deceptive, and I'd felt bad until I thought of all the deception he'd given me over the years.

Calming my hands, I opened the note.

Welcome to the company. You should live like you work for me.

—Greyson Tides

My shaking stopped, and my mouth gaped. Greyson Tides, the mysterious mogul I'd yet to meet. He was elusive from everything I'd heard, so why did he care if I had nice things in my apartment? My intrigue about him grew as I looked around, completely bewildered.

Sitting in the chair, I tried to catch my breath now that I knew my life wasn't being upended again. That Mason hadn't found me. That *he* hadn't found me. The pressure of it all, the way the fear had squeezed my lungs until they'd been devoid of air, the emptiness that filled the rest of me when the fear wasn't overwhelming me, hit me like a thousand bricks landing on my shoulders and I collapsed from the weight. Tears fell. Ones I'd been holding at bay since the moment I'd decided to run from the truth, from the world Mason had hidden me in, from the man who had opened my eyes to it. I cried for everything I'd lost and everything I missed. I cried for the gesture of kindness from a man

I didn't even know, one whose action helped to assuage the pain men had been causing me lately.

When the tears stopped, I left my soggy fries and curled into the soft, welcoming bed, wanting the day to end and wishing I could go back to the life I'd left, knowing I never could. Doing so would only bring me more pain.

THE NEXT MORNING, I familiarized myself with my newly decorated apartment. There was nothing I could find that I didn't love about it. From the tiniest detailed flowers that were stenciled onto the cream paint to the fairy lights that surrounded the bed. As I nibbled on a chocolate chip muffin I'd found in my stocked cabinets—full of my favorite snacks—there was a knock on the door.

I froze, my hand lingering mid-air with a chunk of muffin. What if it was Greyson Tides? And why did that thought send tingles through my body? I didn't even know what the man looked like or anything about him, yet even the thought of him excited me.

"Shit, Riley. Don't be stupid. He's probably some old balding man with a potbelly and grandkids," I muttered.

Opening the door, I found Ava looking back at me and not the hunky version of Greyson Tides I was trying to convince myself didn't exist.

"Holy shit! Who do I have to blow to get this in my apartment?"

I crossed my arms, not sure how I felt about someone I didn't even know assuming I'd dropped to my knees for some sugar daddy.

"Oh, sorry. Not implying you did that," she said, holding her hands up.

"Thank you, because I didn't." Although the thought of dropping to my knees and having Greyson Tides as my sugar daddy didn't make me as uncomfortable as it should have. *Old man with grandkids, Riley,* I reminded myself, pushing the image from my head.

"What happened to your plethora of furniture?" Ava asked, looking around.

"I sold it. I was planning to shop for new stuff today but..." How did I explain the generous offer that seemed to hold its own implications now that I had to say it out loud? I didn't think redecorating apartments came without a cost, nor that it was something normal for new employees. I was sure Ken didn't get the same perk when he joined the firm. The thought should have left me unnerved, but anticipation shivered through me instead.

"But?" she asked, taking in my new digs.

"It was part of my sign-on bonus at the firm."

"Damn. What firm is that and how do I get a job there?" She sat at the table, her ripped jeans exposing her entire kneecap. Today she had a streak of pink going through her blonde curls, which she'd tied in two ponytails. She wore a long-sleeved black shirt with the words 'suck it or f*ck it' on the front.

I could only imagine Mason's reaction to her. He was so in control, so particular about his image and the brands he wore. Ava was nothing like anyone he would have let me hang out with. He'd always vetted my friends, steering me toward the more elite ones. I rebelled with the men I dated, which drove him crazy, and now that I knew who he really was, I understood why they always left and broke my heart. It wasn't until the last one that I'd been smart enough to hide it from him. But it was the last one who had shattered me completely and left Mason falsely assured that I would never rebel again.

"I'm a financial planner," I told Ava. "I work in the Tides Building on 22nd." After my first day, I discovered that the building had a name, and I was the only one in the city who didn't know who owned it.

"You work for Greyson Tides?" Her eyes had gone wide, and she said his name in a hush.

"I suppose you could say that. I've never met him, but he owns the firm and apparently the building," I said with a shrug.

"And everything else in the city."

"Do you know him?"

Her laugh was loud and accompanied by a snort. "I don't hang with that crowd. Although I'm not sure he has a crowd. He's pretty aloof, keeps to himself. I've never seen him."

"Huh." My infatuation with a man I'd never met was growing, and I didn't know what to make of it.

"I don't have to go into work until six tonight. I'm procrastinating and looking for an excuse to get out. Got any plans?"

I gave her a smile. "Nope, just a lot of cash to spend from selling my furniture and a need to spend it. Is there shopping in town?"

"Is there ever," she said, her eyes bright with excitement. "Come on, I'll help you spend that money."

She didn't give me time to say no, hopping up and telling me to be ready in twenty minutes. Sighing, I took a quick shower and dressed. Since I hadn't bothered washing my hair, I was trying to get it to do anything cute when Ava returned.

"Here," she said, dropping her purse and snatching my brush from my hand.

After rummaging through my bathroom, she returned with some bobby pins and proceeded to pile my hair up so that I looked like I'd spent an hour getting it styled. I peered at it in the mirror, wondering why it never looked that cute when I fixed it.

"I did a stint at a hair salon before I decided to go to grad school," she admitted with a shrug. "I learned a few tricks while I was answering the phone and sweeping up."

"I'd say you learned a lot of tricks. This is fantastic. Can you do my hair every morning?"

With a laugh, she handed me my coat and headed for the door. "I'll give you a few pointers," she said as we headed out of the building.

We chatted as we made our way uptown to the shopping district. Bridgeville was an enormous city, divided into districts. There was the financial or business district where I worked, the shopping district, which was home to boutique stores and name brand stores that catered to the more affluent shoppers, and a food district where local bars and eateries lined the streets. There were, of course, exceptions, like my coffee shop and small shops and restaurants that were more geared to the locals. As Ava and I hopped from store to store, my hands filling increasingly with bags, I got to know her better, discovering that bartending was a side gig to help with books and supplies she needed for school. After graduating with a degree in art history, she'd taken four years off to travel and work before pursuing her graduate degree.

"Does bartending pay enough to cover tuition?" I asked, chomping on a hotdog from a street vendor.

"No," she said, moving a napkin just in time to catch the mustard that fell from it. I gave her a smile through my chews. "My uncle lives here, and he offered to pay for school if I came to Bridgeville."

"That's really nice. Do you get to see him often?"

"Nah, he works all the time. He's far up in the company he works for, so I rarely see him." She wiped her mouth on the back of her sleeve, laughing when she caught my grimace. "I know, that's not very ladylike."

"No, it's not," I said, joining her laugh.

"So what made you move to Bridgeville?" she asked, tossing the end of her hot dog into a trash can.

I froze. Every time I answered that question, it brought back memories and emotions that I couldn't seem to bury. Swallowing,

I replied, "Looking for a change of pace. Treemont is rural and boring. I wanted to try something new." I stared at the remains of my lunch, my appetite lost.

"Did you grow up there?" she asked.

"Yeah, I was born there. It's pretty, but not as exciting as it is here." I was more than ready for a change in conversation. Following her lead, I dropped the rest of my hot dog in the trash and said, "And the shopping here is far better. Ready to hit a few more stores? With your help, my wardrobe is filling up."

Her brown eyes evaluated me for a moment before she shrugged and said, "Ready as I'll ever be. Spending someone else's money is fun."

We spent the rest of the day weighing my arms down with more bags until we were both too exhausted to walk any further and I had enough new clothes for my wardrobe to complete my efforts to rid myself of my old life. It was one more step in distancing myself from Treemont, Mason, and the past that I couldn't seem to shake.

Chapter Five

GREYSON

The week went by slowly, but it gave me time to watch Riley. She was predictable, which was something I hadn't expected. It surprised me that a sister of Mason Brinks would be that way. If she'd been my sister, I would have trained her to stay unpredictable. But she wasn't my sister. She was my prey.

I followed her, always staying a few steps behind, far enough for her not to notice me, but close enough to smell the perfume she wore and hear the click of her heels as she walked. There was something about the way she flipped her hair when she wore it down that left my dick hard and had me yearning to thread my fingers through it. I wasn't certain she was the type who liked it pulled, and even if she was, I wasn't certain I'd want to. There was something about Riley that caused a different reaction in me than I usually had to women. It wasn't a need to dominate her, although it was only a matter of time before I would own her. This was a need just to touch her. A craving to feel her body and to hear her cries. I wiped my hand down my face, irritated that I was going soft when this wasn't about bringing her pleasure. It was about making her suffer for my pleasure. It didn't matter if she didn't like her hair pulled, she'd learn to like it.

After Sherry purchased the furniture Riley had brought with her, I went through it for any small touches of her to keep before I sent it on to be donated. There'd been only a few tokens, an earring lodged in the corner of a drawer, a bent bookmark, and an old tube of strawberry lip gloss. I twirled the tube in my hand, wondering what it tasted like on her lips. She had plump lips that looked perfect for kissing or taking my cock. She didn't strike me as the kind of girl who enjoyed being on her knees either, but that would change as well. Because if I was going to destroy her brother, I wanted to tell him how good those lips felt while I fucked his sister's mouth.

I heard the click of her heels in the hall and sat up in my seat. I'd left the office early, needing to be here before she came home. The decorator I'd hired had done exactly what he'd needed to perfect her apartment, and I was looking forward to seeing her expression when she walked in. Anticipation spilled through me as I watched through the camera I'd had installed in her wall and inconspicuously hidden next to a picture. The apartment next door was empty as I'd evicted the tenant the moment I had my building manager offer Riley the studio. It was mine now. My way to watch her every move, to gain insight into every aspect of her life.

She walked in and I sat closer to the camera, seeing her stunned expression and hearing her gasp. I imagined what that gasp would sound like when my cock was sinking into her and shook the thought away. There was no reason for me to be so excited about her reaction, like it mattered to me if she liked what I'd given her. But I was and when I saw the shake in her hands, the fear that filled her eyes as she scanned the room, the disappointment was heavy. She didn't like it. I tried to shake off the letdown, to remember that this was part of the game, but the sensation didn't fade.

When she found my note, my nerves grew. Nothing made me nervous. I was a man to be feared. I knew no fear, but in that moment, my heart pounded as I held my breath. Relief came over her expression and the tension in her shoulders released. The reaction made me curious as to why she'd had the initial response. She was afraid of something, and I wondered if that something had to do with what she was running from.

I needed to find out, but nothing I'd found so far gave me the answers. She flopped into the chair at the small table and cried. My spirit dropped, my mouth going dry as I swallowed back the defeat that was mounting in my chest. This wasn't the way she was supposed to have reacted, and I felt crushed at having made her cry.

I stood, running my hand through my hair and cursing. Why did I care if she cried? I was here to hurt her. To lift her up and drop her so she shattered. Maybe I'd expected her to appreciate my gesture of kindness, but this reaction should have made me happy. She was in tears. That's what this was about. Breaking her. Her tears should have left me elated. But they didn't, and that had me confounded.

I exited the apartment, storming off and trying to fathom why Riley Brinks was twisting my emotions when I'd only just begun my game.

MY NIGHTS WERE USUALLY LONG. Over the years I'd played, burying the loneliness in women or alcohol, but as I aged, my tastes changed, and I found that most women didn't have what I wanted, and only high-end liquor quenched my thirst. I'd never been a partier, knowing it put me at risk, and in time, I closed myself off to only satisfying my hungers on rare occasions, never getting close enough to any woman to make one a habit.

Riley was a woman I wanted, one who was getting to me with each subtle move she made and every step further in my game she took. I shouldn't have been getting closer to her. I should have walked away because she was becoming a habit, a need, an obsession I couldn't force from my mind.

I spent that Friday evening in my home office, staring at the camera on my phone and watching her sleep. The fairy lights over her bed left a soft glow that lingered on her body as she tossed and turned. I'd fallen asleep to the sight, waking the next morning to find my phone still in my hand, my head on my desk.

Stretching the stiffness from my shoulders and straightening my back, I turned the camera off and showered. She'd still been asleep when I rose, the blankets thrown aside so that I had a fantastic view of her tiny black panties curving over her ass, and her bare back where her tank top had pushed up as she slept. I wanted to touch her so desperately that my cock ached thinking about it. Toweling my hair dry, I debated going to the apartment so I could watch her further. The camera on my phone worked when I couldn't be there and I could have set a bigger one up in my house rather than the apartment, but I liked the idea of being so close to her when I watched. Knowing she was right next door added a thrill to my game.

It was Saturday, though, and I was hoping her schedule was less predictable on a weekend. If it was, there was a risk to stepping foot in her building. Plus, the floor wasn't empty. She had Ava living across the hall. I could have evicted her like I had the other tenant, but Ava was a favor. She was my henchman's niece and Den had worked for me since the beginning. I let her stay there for an insignificant rent that she wouldn't find anywhere else. Since she worked a late shift, she wasn't a threat to my plans, but I still didn't want to chance being seen anywhere near Riley's apartment.

I gazed at my phone, that desire to look at Riley screaming

uncontrollably. Unable to resist, I turned the camera on, seeing her at the table with Ava.

"Fuck," I muttered. Ava didn't know me, nor did she know my connection to her uncle and that I had anything to do with the building or her rent. But I didn't like how they were chatting away as if they were best friends. A streak of jealousy slithered through me, and I shook it off. It was ridiculous to think Riley wouldn't interact with other people. But I wanted that interaction to be mine. To have her smile and laugh reserved for me.

Slamming the phone down, I ran my hands through my hair. What had gotten into me? This was out of hand, and I needed to step away before I lost control. Grabbing my phone, I closed out of the camera and tucked it in my pocket. I finished getting ready and made my way out of the house, determined to get my mind from Riley and back to the controlled, calculated man I had always been.

I drove through town, heading to the jewelers on the shadier end. This was an area I rarely frequented, keeping my more questionable dealings on the low and letting Den run them. But I needed a reprieve from my obsession with Riley. The further I drove from her, the calmer I became, although the urge to stop and look at my camera constantly nudged at me. I ignored it. Before I'd closed out of the camera, I'd heard them talking about shopping, so I suspected Riley wouldn't even be there.

At least she was doing something sporadic, something that didn't involve work or her apartment. I had yet to see her do more than walk through the city and surrounding neighborhoods. Sometimes I'd follow her, staying far enough behind that she didn't notice me, and observing the way she took things in as if everything was fresh and new. She looked at every detail, from an icicle to a dog print in fresh snow, and I loved watching the wonder in her eyes, the sweet way she smiled at strangers she passed on the street or stooped to pet a dog walking by.

Even with how cold the weather had turned toward the end of

the week, she still wandered out on her lunch break, her head tipped toward the snowflakes as they fell in her dark hair.

I turned into the back lot, my guys pulling in behind me just as I exited the car. In my younger days, I would have let them drive me everywhere, but now I drove myself, a statement of how secure I was in my position of power. Rarely did I let them drive me now. Giving them a nod, I made my way to the rear of the jewelry shop.

"Boss," Den said, greeting me immediately. "You checking up on me?"

"I have to keep you on your toes, Den." I rolled my neck as I walked down the stairs, nodding to Frank as he moved aside.

"If I didn't know better, I'd say you're bored," Den observed from behind me.

I stopped and turned slowly to him. Any other man would have stepped away in fear, but Den had been by my side since the beginning and nothing frightened him, not even me. He stared me down, arms crossed over his broad chest.

"But I know better, although I have to say, Greyson, I haven't seen you this rattled in a long time."

I sneered, seeing Frank step back from my periphery.

"Nothing rattles me, Den. You should know that."

"I do, which is why you're going to tell me what the fuck is going on."

I glanced at Frank and turned my back on Den, walking into the shop. Most of my investments were in real estate but I divested some of my money in side projects, including the bars in the city and a few underground gambling facilities. Frank ran the money from the gambling tables through the jewelry store, which was a front. Cash lined the tables in bundles, a few of the guys bundling it before it would go to the next stop.

I headed into the small office in the back and slammed the door once Den was through. Grabbing him by the collar, I threw him against the wall, the fake wood paneling shaking with the impact.

"Never call me out in front of the men again, Den."

He smirked, and I let go of his collar, flexing my arms and feeling the muscles press against my button-down dress shirt.

"Fuck, you are stressed. Is it the girl?"

"She's not a girl," I hissed, hating the sound.

"The woman, then?" he corrected with a laugh.

"Fuck off."

"Shit, I haven't seen you this affected by a woman in...damn, never."

I glared at him, not caring to talk about the obsessive cravings I was having for Riley Brinks.

"You said you were playing with her, boss. Not anything more. Ruin her and send her back to Brinks in a body bag."

The thought nearly destroyed me, and I gripped my fists. His eyes flickered downward, noting my tension.

"Fuck. Don't tell me you're falling for her, Greyson. That's bad."

"I'm not falling for her," I said, running my hands through my hair.

"She's the enemy's sister. The perfect target. Or are you forgetting your own words when you gave her even more incentive to move here?"

"I'm not forgetting. There are just...complications."

"Like what? How you decorated her apartment? Gave her that nice window office after kicking her colleague to another office? Destroy and return. That's the goal. Taking down Brinks so he never thinks about fucking with you again."

"I know that."

"Do you?"

Rolling my neck, I clenched my jaw, smoothing my hand down my shirt and ensuring it no longer showed the wrinkled evidence of my loss of control. "Of course I do. Stop badgering me like you're in charge. I'm the one in charge. This is my show, not yours."

"Good. I told you when we started out in this business, I don't want to be in charge. I'm along for the ride." He moved aside so I could leave the office but put his hand on the door as I reached for the doorknob. "I've known you a long time, boss. This woman has you out of sorts."

"Maybe."

"Maybe? I don't think so. Is this the one to break you?" He gave me a coy grin, his brown eyes full of mischief.

"Wipe that damned smirk off your face before I punch it off. And get the fuck out of my way."

He moved and let me leave, his laugh trailing me. If anyone knew me well enough to know Riley was breaking me, it would be him. I cursed myself for letting him see my weakness, although he was the only one I trusted enough to let in.

My phone buzzed, and I pulled it out to read the text as I walked back through the shop.

I think she will break you, and I'm going to be here to enjoy the show.

Fucking prick, I texted him in return, biting back my chuckle and covering it with my sternest look.

As I got in my car, I scolded myself for not staying home and hiding my lack of control. Unable to resist, I turned the camera on, hating the disappointment that filled my chest upon discovering that Riley wasn't there. And questioning why that ache in my chest was growing more constant.

Chapter Six

RILEY

After my long day of shopping with Ava, I was thankful my new apartment décor came with a wardrobe because my small closet wouldn't have held the new clothes I bought while we were out. I spent Saturday night cleaning out my old clothes, ready to embrace the new. At one point, I found the scarves that my mother had brought back with her when she'd accompanied my father on one of his business trips. I'd only been about five at the time and the rich colors of the waist-length silk scarves had fascinated me. Mason would scold me for sneaking into her closet and playing dress up with them.

I was ten when my parents died, and the courts gave Mason custody of me. He'd been old enough and my parents had left enough money to care for me. I hadn't realized he'd built his own network by then and likely influenced the courts to let him take care of me. I'd never questioned why anyone would give a nineteen-year-old custody of his ten-year-old sister. As we'd been cleaning their things out, Mason had found the scarves and given them to me. They were a piece of my mother, a memory that I cherished, even if Mason's touch now tarnished them.

I hung the scarves around the corner of my headboard, liking how the colors caught in the fairy lights.

The rest of the weekend, I scouted the city, checking out the local restaurants and familiarizing myself with streets I hadn't ventured down. It amazed me that even with all the people in this city, I was still as lonely as I had been in Treemont. Ava was only one person out of thousands, and although I kept looking, I hadn't bumped into the kind stranger again. I was still angry at myself for not getting his name and number.

What did it matter? My track record with men was sketchy, and he probably had a wife and kids. Besides, my mind kept wandering to the elusive Greyson Tides, already giving him a personality and a rock-hard body to go along with the sexy voice that filled my fantasies. There wasn't a man who could compete with that, no matter that I kept telling myself he was likely the exact opposite.

I walked into the office on Monday morning with my mind on nothing as my cup of coffee warmed my hands. Snow was falling, the bitter cold of winter in this part of the province reminding me how much I missed Treemont. I stopped to say good morning to Matt at the front of the office when the doors to the building opened and a burly man walked in, taking a protective stance next to the door. Within seconds, in rushed my good Samaritan, followed by another massive man whose eyes scanned the lobby before he took a position on the other side of the door. I stared, wide-eyed, at the man who had left a lasting impression on me, even though I hadn't seen him since he'd handed me back my purse and flashed me that gorgeous smile. My body grew warm as he glanced my way, those dark blue eyes stealing my breath. He didn't stop, didn't say hello. He simply gave me a sly grin and continued walking. My eyes followed him as he got into the private elevator at the far end of the office. He kept his eyes on me, that penetrating gaze leaving me drenched by the time the door closed.

"Who was that?" I asked Matt once my brain started working again.

"Greyson Tides? You don't know who Greyson Tides is after a week here?"

I drew my eyes from the elevator and looked questioningly at Matt, my heart thudding.

"Greyson Tides? That was him?"

"You need to get out, Riley."

Greyson Tides, the owner of the firm, the most powerful man in the city, had been my savior that first day here. My knees nearly gave out when I realized he'd been the same one who had filled my apartment so wonderfully. I pondered if he'd known it was me.

"Does he ever come down here?" I asked, trying not to seem obvious about the obsession that was mounting in my mind. The one that had already grown dangerous as I'd made him into something that was very close to the real-life version.

"No, he stays in his office when he's here. And we're barred from it. There's a keycard for the penthouse office, so don't get any ideas. Every woman in this office drools when Greyson Tides walks through, but he doesn't give them any notice. Keeps to himself." He shook his head. "One girl tried sneaking up there before they installed the keycard. They fired her on the spot. His security goons escorted her out and shipped her stuff to her."

"He doesn't play, does he?"

"No, and it doesn't pay to get involved with Greyson Tides." He moved in closer to me, whispering, "He's a dangerous man and he owns everything and everyone in Bridgeville."

Matt walked away, leaving me to reconcile the version of the man who had rescued the purse of a random stranger and walked her to the coffee shop her first day with the image of the reclusive businessman. I bit my lip, staring at the elevator and wishing I could get another glimpse of those heart-stopping blue eyes or hear the way his deep baritone drifted down my spine like a sensual touch.

To my dismay, the rest of my day was dull, dragging painfully slow. I was working with clients now, which lent some speed to the time, but when I wasn't busy discussing finances, I was thinking of Greyson Tides. I couldn't get him off my mind. The way those blue eyes had seen deep into my soul and how that smirk he'd given me had made my legs twist with want. If I was obsessed with him before, it had only grown two-fold.

"Riley." Beth interrupted my thoughts. She was a sweet woman, a few years older than me, with strawberry hair and big green eyes. "We're grabbing drinks at happy hour. Come with us. Matt says you need to get out more."

I laughed, knowing it was the truth. Maybe a drink would help take my mind off Greyson Tides. At least, that was my hope. But by the time I'd had two drinks and binged on enough nachos to feed a football team, he was still in my thoughts. Yawning, I called it a night, pulling my coat on as I said my goodbyes.

"I'll walk you home," Matt said, grabbing his coat as I wrapped my scarf around my neck.

"That's okay, I can manage."

"She who didn't even know the company head when he walked by thinks she can find her way home," he teased.

"You didn't know Mr. Tides?" Beth said, leaning in as she said his name. "The god of Bridgeville."

"God of Bridgeville?" I asked.

"The man is a walking god. He's gorgeous," she said, a blush filling her cheeks.

"Aren't you married with a kid?" said Rick, another colleague.

"That doesn't mean I'm blind," she replied, sticking her tongue out at him. "I can look, I just can't touch."

Laughing, I answered her question, saying, "No, I didn't know who he was."

"She does now," Matt said.

Yes, I did, and now the man was back on my mind again. "If

you insist on walking me home, let's get moving and no more talk about Greyson Tides."

"Thank you!" he said. "That's all any woman seems to talk about around here."

Beth rolled her eyes, and we said goodbye before Matt led me out. His company was pleasant, and we chatted the entire way to my apartment.

"You know," Matt said as we arrived in front of my building. "The company frowns on dating between colleagues, but if you ever want to, I'd be up for taking you out. Show you the city at night, maybe have dinner at a restaurant that doesn't offer your usual fries and diet soda."

"Are you asking me out after you just told me there's no dating allowed?" I sensed the color creep into my cheeks.

He shrugged. "I'm a bit of a rule breaker."

"I'll think about taking you up on the offer. But...I'm not sure that will be anytime soon. I just got out of a...relationship and I'm not ready." Just saying the words brought the emotions forward. It had been nine months, but the hurt and betrayal still seemed raw.

He raised his hands. "No pressure. Just putting it out there. Hopefully, this won't make it weird tomorrow."

"It won't," I said, giving him a smile before heading in.

I couldn't believe he'd asked me out. Matt was a nice guy, and it probably would have been something good for me. Nice guys were never the ones I ended up with, however, and given my current circumstances, I didn't want to entangle anyone in my life, especially anyone who could get hurt. Or anyone who wasn't Greyson Tides.

And he was back on my mind again. "Dammit," I muttered.

Throwing my coat on the chair, I got ready for bed, changing into my jammies—the standard tank top and undies I always wore. Climbing into bed, I stared at the ceiling, my mind still on Greyson Tides. He was in my brain, and I couldn't get him out.

There was something sexy about his eyes, about the way he carried himself. Power oozed from him. Sex oozed from him. Even his voice that day had made its way into my body and found a place to stay.

I hadn't had sex in ages, swearing off men after the last fiasco. I'd been too fearful of getting hurt again. Not that there had been any way to even meet a man other than Mason's men. He had locked me down, his men guarding me to and from work, watching my every move until the night I'd run away. He'd even moved me into his guesthouse for those months, my furniture put in storage after he forced me to give up my apartment. I'd found that storage unit and hired movers to move it all to Bridgeville. It had taken plenty of sneaking around to do, but I'd succeeded.

Sighing, I brushed my hand over my breast, wishing I'd invited Matt up to satisfy the need that seeing Greyson Tides had infected me with. Although I wasn't certain anyone could satisfy it. My stomach clenched as I thought of Greyson's dark eyes and those large hands touching my body. Imagined that seductive voice whispering in my ear as he threaded his hand through my hair. He looked like he would be the perfect balance of commanding power, enough to pull my hair in just the right way to drench me.

The thought set me on fire, and I cupped my breast, rubbing my nipple between my fingers while imagining it was his fingers. My stomach trembled, warmth growing between my legs. I kicked the blankets from my body, my other hand sliding below my underwear. Closing my eyes, I pictured his hands roaming my body, and I bit my lip, a soft moan slipping through my teeth. My fingers hit my arousal, spreading it over my clit. I clenched my legs, drawing my knee up and sinking my finger in, wishing it was him filling me instead. I imagined his touch, firm and forceful, those blue eyes breaking me as his hand held my neck, constricting my breath. The thought had me arching my back, and I tipped my head, rubbing my clit as my climax built. I pinched my nipple, tugging it as I drove my finger further. Pulling it back out to my clit, I rubbed along it, growing wetter the closer I grew to release. Plunging two fingers in, I cried out, my orgasm ripping through me. My legs crossed as the waves rippled and I envisioned Greyson Tides climaxing with me, his hands squeezing my hips tight as he growled my name.

When the force of my release waned, I relaxed, bringing my hand back up. Closing my eyes, I wondered why a man I'd seen twice had this effect on me and if I could refrain from blushing at my dirty thoughts the next time I encountered him.

GREYSON

R iley's weekend had given me more insight into her, yet still not enough to get close to her. I spent Saturday night in the apartment next door, watching as she weeded through her clothes, enjoying the show when she started trying on the new clothes she'd bought. Sexy skirts with slits that showed her luscious thighs, a dress that left no doubt her curves were ones I wanted, and blouses that dipped to the swell of her breasts. Watching her had me enthralled and I couldn't will myself to leave until she'd ended the night by laying a handful of long silk scarves over the edge of her headboard. My mind had gone immediately to how she'd look with them tied around her wrists as I fucked her, and it was then that I knew I'd lost it. My reason for spying on her, for needing to be close to her and own her, had turned from revenge to a craving I couldn't stop.

I left after she fell asleep, sneaking from the building and vowing to stop this madness before she derailed my plans.

The rest of the weekend, I avoided getting near Riley, burying myself in my work, and leaving the camera on my phone turned off. I forced myself not to think of her, to leave all thoughts of my plan, of revenge, of her brother, of her aside until I was back in control.

By Monday, I felt more like myself. Venturing into the building later than normal, I saw her there, talking to Matt, the bastard openly flirting with her. I'd have to do something about him. He was already on my radar for prior violations and seeing him talking to Riley left me with no reservations about keeping an even closer eye on him.

He was mid-sentence when Riley turned her emerald eyes to me. My step almost faltered, my heart pounding erratically as recognition filled her face. I lifted my sight to her and cocked a sideways grin as I walked by, not giving her any more notice. This was my game, and I was in control again, even if every part of me wanted to bend her over that desk and fuck her. I'd have my chance.

As the elevator door closed, I let out a sigh of relief that I'd maintained my composure, not letting that craving for her over-take my senses again. I needed Riley in my hands, but not until I was ready. And when I was, there would be no stopping me because I wanted Riley Brinks and from the look in those hungry green eyes, she was mine for the taking.

THAT BROWN-NOSING jackass Matt was hitting on Riley, and I wanted to punch his snotty little nose and wipe his blood up with his face. Insisting my men didn't need to accompany me, I'd followed Riley after she left the office, curious when she'd agreed to go out for drinks with her co-workers. I had no doubt my men were still trailing me, not taking a chance, but this game was mine alone.

There was no risk of Riley finding anything out about me from her co-workers other than what I allowed to be shared.

There was a respective fear of me in my city and that's the way I preferred it. I kept to myself, kept my business associates close to the cuff, and my dealings underground. Businesses like the firm Riley worked in were to keep my head above water and prevented the government cronies from getting too nosy. As it stood, people like me ran the province, our territories divided among separate families. We didn't venture into each other's territories unless it was necessary. And when we did, as Mason Brinks had, it stirred trouble. Some retaliated swiftly. Others, like me, took their time. Riley was me taking my time.

Hidden in the shadows, watching them, my jaw clenched when Matt asked her out. My fists were wound so tight I thought about killing him before he could make it home. Rolling my neck, I listened to her response, letting my breath out when she gently turned him down. Her words caught my attention. She was fresh out of a relationship? That was news to me. Nothing I'd found said she'd dated anyone in over a year. Her brother had to have buried it or kept it under wraps. But why? My mind had more questions than I liked.

I waited until Matt left before I entered the building, keeping far enough back that she'd have time to enter her apartment without seeing me enter the one next door. Letting the tension from earlier fall from my muscles, I sat, watching her through the camera. I should have set it up in my home, but there was more excitement to sitting unseen next door to her and the camera on my phone sufficed when I couldn't get there.

Her clothes came off and, as happened each time I'd seen her strip, my cock lurched. She had a tight body with curves that made me drool. Tonight she wore a black lace thong and when she walked, her ass jiggled invitingly. Fantasies of sinking my dick into that ass flashed through my mind until she turned and her perky tits were in my view. I wiped my hand down my face, trying to get a grip and wondering why I was torturing myself this way. My initial intention had been to find out more about her—her likes, habits, and movements. Instead, all I'd done was give myself a raging hard-on each time I watched her.

Riley pulled on a black tank top, and disappointment filled me until her ass turned back to me. She disappeared into the bathroom for a few minutes, and I took the time to slow my breaths and calm my body.

When she emerged, her hair was in two braids, giving her a girlish look that did nothing to settle my dick as I imagined grabbing them as I fucked her face.

"Shit, Grey," I muttered, sitting back and watching her crawl into bed.

I'd had my decorator situate the bed so that it was directly across from me, the window behind her. The full moon shone in, lighting her body as she lay there. I stared for a few more minutes, readying myself to leave, when her hand moved up her shirt. I sat back into my seat, my jaw dropping. The sheets moved as her other hand lowered below them. She was touching herself, and my dick jerked angrily against my zipper. She kicked the sheets down, giving me the perfect view of her spread legs and those fingers as they moved below her tiny panties.

My fists bunched, and I resisted stroking myself while I watched, mesmerized by the sight. She tightened her legs around her hand, then drew her knee up, her back arching. I could tell she had dipped her fingers deeper, and my dick throbbed, wanting desperately to replace her fingers. Her thighs quivered, tightening around her hand, my eyes going wide as she came, her whimpers filling the room. She'd left me enraptured, my entire body wanting to burst through the wall and fuck her. It was the most erotic thing I'd ever witnessed. I couldn't tear my eyes from her body as she relaxed, her hand moving from below her panties. She flopped her arm over her face and, in time, drifted to sleep.

Sitting back, I stroked my aching cock before convincing myself to leave. I needed to remain in control, and that sight had almost unraveled me. Had she been thinking of that asshole Matt?

The thought threatened to burn me from the inside out. Pushing away thoughts of murdering him violently, I drove home and ran a shower to calm myself. It didn't keep my thoughts from turning to Riley and her writhing body. The need to make her mine, to claim that body for myself, raked through me and I grabbed my cock, stroking it as I imagined sinking into her. Thinking of how wet she likely was as she'd touched herself, I stroked to the same rhythm she'd taken with her fingers. I leaned my other hand on the tile wall and increased my movements, pumping with the ferocity of the images that were berating me until I spilled over the shower floor, wishing my hand was Riley gripping around me as she came undone.

Catching my breath, I rested my head against the tile. My legs were shaking. I hadn't come that hard in a very long time, nor had any woman worked me up the way Riley had. My need for vengeance was turning into an obsession. One I didn't know if I could control. One that had begun the day I'd dared talk to her, to look into those sage eyes and let her ensnare me before I could further weave my web.

I left the shower, toweling off before throwing a pair of boxers on and dropping into a chair, phone in hand. I deliberated calling her brother and telling him to come get her. To take her from my city and from my grasp. But I didn't think that would help at this point. She could be across the world, and I would still crave her.

I hit the camera instead, stroking my calming dick as I watched her sleep, then chastising myself for the behavior until I heard her mumble in her sleep. It was a quiet, breathless sound that resounded through my chest like a thundering storm. "Greyson."

The sun beamed over my face, waking me, and I blinked against the brightness. Heat rose in my cheeks as I thought of how I'd touched myself while envisioning Greyson Tides. He'd plagued my dreams, his eyes, that smirk, the confidence all insinuating their way into my sleep and leaving me even further contented by the time I woke. I didn't want to sleep in today and given how my mind was already playing scenes of chance encounters with Greyson Tides, I knew going back to sleep was not an option. Instead, I took my time getting ready, munching on my bagel as curiosity about Greyson Tides nagged at me.

After cleaning up my breakfast, I dug through my purse and pulled out the cellphone my brother had given me for Christmas last year. I'd turned its tracking off when I left and had powered it down, knowing he would likely still locate me through it even if the tracker was off. I should have left it in Treemont, but there was something about leaving it behind that had seemed like cutting the last connection to him off, and I wasn't ready for that. Plugging it in, but leaving it off still, I sat on my new loveseat, tucking my feet under me as I stared at it.

I missed my brother. Mason and I had always been close... until I'd discovered the lies and the life of deception he'd woven. Dropping my head back, I stared at the ceiling, thinking about the last time I'd seen him. He'd been in his kitchen, his tie undone as he read the paper and sipped on his coffee, not bothering to sit because that was how he was. His green eyes that matched my own had risen, and he'd given me a questioning look. It was the first time I'd talked to him since the truth had come out, even after he insisted I move into the guest house. Ignoring him had become a habit.

It was the morning I left. I'd been waiting for him to head out before I packed up what little I had on me. I'd arranged for the movers to move my things from the storage unit discreetly and prayed he didn't find out until it was too late.

"You finally talking to me?" he'd asked, dropping his cup in the sink and folding his paper.

It had hurt to leave him, but then, he'd hurt me, and the lies he'd fed me all those years had hurt me in ways I didn't think he'd expected. If I'd known the truth, I might have protected myself, but he was my big brother and I supposed he felt he needed to protect me. He hadn't, and what had happened had left me fractured.

"Not necessarily," I replied, my tone sharp.

"Well, you need to. Get over it, Ri. It's time to accept the truth and come into the fold."

"The fold? You mean the criminal shit you and your guys do? You want me to be part of that? After all that happened, you think I'd even consider it?"

He flinched, and I knew the reminder of what had happened hurt him. He turned his back on me and grabbed his sunglasses.

"Christmas is in a month. Let me know what you want."

My mouth had dropped at the sudden change in subject. Like we were done with the situation. He was, but I wasn't. "What do you want?" I asked.

He turned to me, his eyes softer. "My sister back."

He hadn't given me time to respond, walking from the kitchen before I could. I'd stood there, fighting the tears because I knew my next move would crush him. The front door opened, and his car drove off minutes later. For a moment, I'd almost wavered, almost called it off. But I hadn't, and here I was. I hadn't even stayed for Thanksgiving, driving straight through and crying the entire day.

I shoved the memory away. It hurt too much to dwell on the past. Chewing my lower lip, I grabbed the phone and put it into my purse before I threw my shoes on and headed to work.

My mind was still on Mason when I dropped my stuff in my office and stumbled to the lobby for a cup of the bland coffee we offered clients. I caught sight of Greyson Tides as he walked to the elevator, his head lowered while he looked at his phone. The two men I suspected were his security were still at the front door, looking out at something on the street. Instinct driving me, my mindset not where it should have been, I ran to the elevator and jumped in just as the doors closed. He looked up at me, his eyes wide until they narrowed. It was too late to back out now; the doors were closed, and the floors were climbing.

I swallowed awkwardly loud, lost in those blue eyes, flashes of my previous nights' escapades with my fingers clouding my ability to focus. My voice fled, reality hitting me that I'd just made a foolish move that would likely cost me my job.

He reached over and hit the emergency button, the elevator jolting to a halt. His eyes never left me, and their intensity made my knees weak.

"I'm waiting," he said, his voice terse and hard, as if he wasn't the same man who had knocked me over with his smile on the sidewalk that day.

"I...I wanted to thank you," I said, finally finding my voice and wondering why I sounded so meek.

"For?" He raised a brow, and I could see he knew exactly what for, but he wanted me to say it.

"For the furniture and the other things you sent me. They were perfect."

He tilted his head, studying me, and I couldn't read his eyes. "I thought perhaps you wouldn't like them," he said, his voice softer.

"Oh no, I love everything. I just didn't have any way to tell you."

He stepped closer to me, putting his phone in his coat pocket. I couldn't help taking a step back, hitting the wall. Warmth spread through my body at his closeness.

"Did you know it was me?" I asked, not sure how to react to his proximity and the penetrating gaze that was melting my insides. "That day on the street?"

He gave me a crooked grin, and my legs quivered.

"No." He stepped further into my space, and I could smell his cologne. It was a masculine scent that spoke of power and strength, and I wondered how it would smell with his skin against mine. My lips parted, and his eyes darkened. "Do you know what happens when someone dares enter my elevator?"

I inadvertently let my head fall back against the wall as his hand rested on it above me. There were so many levels of inappropriateness to this situation, but I didn't care.

"I may have heard a rumor," I answered, my confidence returning as I slid my foot up the wall, my knee rubbing against his pants. "But does it depend?"

"On what?" he asked, leaning closer so his body was almost touching mine.

"On the woman." It was a bold statement, but my body was on fire with need for this man. My type had always been the bad boys. That propensity had landed me in trouble with the last one, and my intuition told me that no matter how put together Greyson Tides looked, he was definitely a bad boy.

His hand moved to my leg, pulling it up higher, and I inhaled sharply. His touch was firm, confirming that my fantasies had been correct, and this man would bring me to ecstasy like no other.

"What are you implying, Miss Brinks?" he asked as his hand rose up my thigh, pushing my skirt higher.

"That you don't mind my abrupt invasion of your morning routine."

He reached the edge of my panties, and my heart raced. "I don't mind interruptions, Miss Brinks, but don't make it a habit." He caressed my ass, jerking me against him, my hands going to his chest and loving how hard the muscles were below his clothes.

"And what if I do?"

He dropped his mouth to my ear and whispered, "You won't like the consequences," before he let me go.

I fell against the wall as he released the emergency button and looked away. He glanced back over at me just as the elevator door opened. "Next time, leave the thong at home, Miss Brinks."

He walked off without another word, the door closing and leaving me so shaken I didn't know what else to do but to push the down button.

Matt stared at me when I returned, but the intense stares of the men who had accompanied Greyson were what left me unnerved. They were bodyguards, something I'd failed to realize the first time I'd seen them take their positions at the front of the building. Now that one had his hand strategically placed so that I could see the end of his gun, it was clear. Behind the deadly glare was a spark of humor, one that matched the smirk he wore.

I waited to see if they would grab me and remove me from the building, but neither moved as if Greyson had made an exception for me, one they knew to obey. Relaxing, I gave them a playful smile and walked back into the office space. Greyson Tides was powerful enough to have bodyguards yet confident enough in that power to leave them at the door, something that spoke volumes about the man who had left me soaked within minutes of being in his presence.

"Did you really just run into Mr. Tides' elevator?" Matt asked, his eyes large. His voice was hushed, and his sight kept darting to the bodyguards, waiting for them to come after me.

"I did," I said with a shrug. "I wanted to introduce myself."

The lie came easily, but then I'd learned from the best. I made my way back to my desk, collapsing in my chair just as my legs gave out.

I spent the rest of the day in a fog, unable to do anything but think of the way Greyson's hand had felt on my skin. The way I'd wanted him to continue and fuck me right there against the elevator wall. That touch was enough to take my cravings for him to an entirely different level. I seriously thought about sneaking off to the bathroom to pleasure myself, he'd left me so wet.

THE WEEK WENT by with no other sightings of Greyson Tides. Not that I wasn't looking. In fact, I found every excuse to wander into the lobby just to see him walk by. Every one of my attempts failed.

Ava peeked in my office as I was gathering my things on Friday. She had the night off and had texted me about dinner and drinks. Knowing I needed something to take the edge off and to get my mind off the sexy man who was dominating it, I'd accepted.

"Ready to pick up some men?" she teased.

"Definitely not," I replied, thinking there was only one man I wanted to have pounding me and I was positive no other would satisfy that need. "But I'll take a few drinks and some food. I'm starving."

Beth walked by and I said goodbye. She and the others were going out for happy hour, but they'd left me out this time. The few women I worked with had been distant to me this week, but I couldn't pinpoint why—unless Matt had blabbed about my sprint to the elevator, and the fact that I still had my job had spurred rumors. Jealousy was an ugly thing, but I wasn't about to explain that nothing happened...even if the interaction had been completely inappropriate. The thought sent a tingle through my body.

Ava waved a hand in front of my face. "You still with me?"

Laughing, I pushed it away and grabbed my bag. "I am. Let's go relax."

"And find you a hunk to take home. That apartment needs some masculinity."

I threw her a look. "I'm not bringing a man home."

"A woman then?"

Rolling my eyes, I walked past her. "No one is coming home with me." Because I knew no man would erase the touch of Greyson Tides from my body and I didn't think I wanted it erased.

The small restaurant Ava picked was a few blocks from our apartment building, tucked into a corner where I would never have spotted it. What it lacked in atmosphere, it made up for in food, and I scarfed down my lobster nachos while I listened to Ava drone on about the classes she'd signed up for next semester.

Stabbing a thick piece of lobster meat with my fork, I asked, "Do you know anything about Greyson Tides?"

I had tried to ask nonchalantly, but she wasn't going for it.

"Him again? Didn't we talk about him when you first moved in?"

"Yeah, but I've settled in now and I saw him the other day—"

Her brown eyes grew wide. "You saw him?" She leaned in closer. "What's he look like?"

"He's..." Our moment in the elevator returned to my mind,

the warmth of his hand on my ass and the erection that had pressed against me. "Handsome."

"Handsome? I've heard he's to die for."

"Yeah, you could say that." I stabbed the lobster again, only then realizing I'd shredded the piece so badly there was no way it was going on my fork.

"You stab that plate anymore and it's going to shatter. Tell me more."

She had her elbows on the table, her dish now pushed to the side.

"Why does it matter?"

"Because Greyson Tides is a god in this city, one who is elusive and hard to find. He keeps to himself, and people rarely see him. Only those who work with him or for him ever get to."

Every time I found something more out about him, it only increased my desire for him. From Ava's reaction, I wasn't the only one in this city craving a piece of the man.

"Plus he's loaded. He's a millionaire who owns everything."

I sat back, giving up on the remainder of my food and taking a sip of my wine. "He has gorgeous blue eyes and a voice that could make you come just from hearing it."

Her mouth dropped. "Fuck, you really did see him. You got close enough to talk to him?" A devious smile formed. "Did you come? Or did you masturbate to the memory of him when you got home?"

My cheeks grew warm.

"Holy shit, you did!"

"Ava!" I said in a hush, trying to quiet her down.

"I don't blame you. I would have done the same thing." She was laughing hard, and I really wanted to change the subject. I glanced around, knowing she'd been loud enough for the others in the small restaurant to hear us. We were next to the bar and there were only men close by. One met my eyes, giving me a smirk, and I looked away quickly. Another in the corner had his head tilted my way. Even though he had his hood drawn, I could feel the heaviness of his gaze.

Shrinking down in my seat, I got Ava talking about the bar where she worked, glad to have the conversation of me touching myself to thoughts of Greyson Tides over. Not only was my blush fading too slowly, but he was back on my mind again and I had a feeling I'd be letting my fingers wander when I got home.

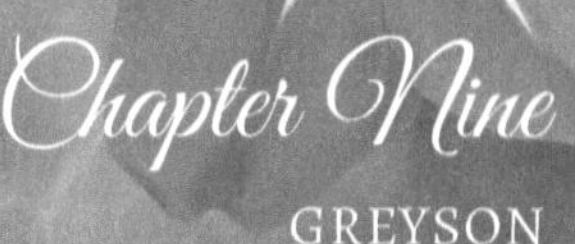

After I left Riley on the elevator, I greeted Sherry quickly and locked myself in my office, resting against the door as I tried to control the whirlwind of uncontrollable emotions going through me. She'd had been right there, daring to step into my elevator. So close that I couldn't resist touching. And she'd wanted it. Every sign she gave me was a welcoming one. Her lips had parted, and it had taken every ounce of control not to kiss her, to push her into that wall and fuck her. Touching her had been a mistake, one that had given me a taste of her I didn't think I could shake. I couldn't stop thinking about the soft skin of her leg that led to the curve of her ass, bare with the edge of her thong teasing me.

This game was getting dangerous, and once again, I questioned if I should stop. I was in too deep on so many levels. When she'd told me she loved the gift I'd given her, my heart had leaped, erasing the disappointment I'd had the day I'd watched her cry over it. I didn't like my reaction to her admission, how uncontrollable it had been, how good it had felt at the time.

Running my hand through my hair, I strode across the office, dropping my coat. I had a choice. I could call this game off and send her packing. Fire her and give her no ability to find work in the city, forcing her to run back to her brother. Or I could continue this game, even with the mounting craving I had for her. I knew I would have her, that I would feel the softness of the rest of her body. I just didn't know if I'd be able to destroy her like I planned or if I'd be able to do anything but crave her more.

The ring of my phone forced my thoughts from her.

"Talk," I answered, seeing that it was Alec.

Alec was the man I used whenever I needed eyes outside the city. He never failed to find information that was buried to keep people like me from seeing it.

"Boss, I dug around again. No boyfriend for over a year. Before that, there was some guy who worked at a local bar, but her brother ran him off. Not up to Mason's standards for his sister."

"Are you sure?" I had given Alec a call after calming down the prior night. It bothered me that Riley had said she'd just gotten out of a relationship. My sources had found no sign of that. As a precaution, I had Alec run through his sources.

"Certain. I do have information you might find interesting, though. I was going to fill you in last night, but I wanted to check one more contact first."

"Go ahead."

"Brinks is losing his shit. Seems he didn't know his sister was leaving."

I sat up straight. He hadn't known. I'd initially thought that he'd sent her here to get to me, but after my first encounter with her, I realized that wasn't the case. She had no idea who I was. Finding out Mason didn't know she was here left me curious. Was she running from him?

"That's an interesting twist. Any idea why?"

"No. But he's tearing the town up hunting for her. And she's not the only one he's hunting. I think one of his men turned on him."

That was news. No one turned on Mason Brinks. Just like no one turned on me. Anyone who dared didn't live to see life outside our worlds.

"Who?"

"One of his henchmen, Clint Randall. Relatively new, so I'm not familiar with him."

"Any idea what he did?"

"No, that's the strange thing. Mason's keeping it under wraps. He's got his closest men hunting for this guy while he and Tyson are hunting for Riley."

Tyson Raines. He was as powerful as Mason only because the two had grown up together. By the time they were in their early twenties, Mason owned his territory, with Tyson by his side. They were best friends and inseparable, and Tyson was a force to fear just as much as Mason was.

"Shit, both of them? That's an issue." If Mason looked to Bridgeville and Tyson followed, it would be war. And I wasn't ready. I wanted Riley in my hands and poised for me to crush her before I dealt with Mason. At least that's what I'd told myself before falling under her spell.

I rubbed my temple, saying, "Keep on it, Alec. I want to know any move he makes. If he as much as looks my way."

"Yes, boss. But wouldn't it be better to just turn her over to him and be done with it?"

No, it wouldn't because I hadn't touched her enough yet. "No, she's running from something, and I have a feeling Brinks is part of that. Until I discover what she knows, her presence here stays silent."

I hung up with Alec, trying to work my mind through the recent developments. So, Mason was hunting his sister and a traitor. I briefly wondered if the two had anything to do with each other. Regardless, I needed to ramp up my game. My insides twisted in anticipation—time to play a little cat and mouse.

Ensuring my people were on alert after hearing the news from

Alec, I left the office early and worked from home for the rest of the day. It gave me time to think and time away from Riley.

I DISTANCED myself from Riley the rest of the week until Friday night. I had planned to search her place, knowing she was going out with Ava after work, but I couldn't resist following the two first. They stopped at a small restaurant a few blocks from her apartment and, curious, I snuck in. I'd left the house incognito, ordering my men to stay put this time. Den had complained, but I couldn't risk anyone spotting them. A black hoodie that I never would have worn covered my head and let me blend into the darkness. I picked a spot at the bar, close enough to their table to listen, but in a shadowed corner where Riley wouldn't notice me.

Ava was a talker, and I could see Riley's attention drifting, her eyes staring out the window at the snow that was just starting. Figuring I'd heard enough to know Ava wasn't talking her into picking up a date for the night, I paid the bartender, intent on returning to my original plan of sneaking into Riley's apartment. Until I heard Riley ask about me. Her voice was hushed, but Ava had already downed a few drinks and her voice carried.

I listened, smiling at Riley's responses. She was curious about me, and I hadn't read her wrong in the elevator. The thought had me hard, and I shifted on my stool, the uncomfortable pressure in my pants only growing as I discovered Riley had been thinking of me when she'd touched herself, confirming my suspicion after hearing her say my name in her sleep. I squeezed my glass so hard that the glass splintered. There was no way I could hold back any longer. I needed to move forward with my plan because she was right where I wanted her. Although, I wasn't so sure where I wanted her anymore, other than with her mouth on my dick. But even that image had shifted. My body craved her in a completely different way now. I wanted to touch her, to feel her body writhing against me as she fell apart.

Fuck, I needed to leave. Pulling my hood up further, I left the bar, walking so close to Riley I could smell her perfume. It sent my blood pulsing with need that didn't fade until the further I was from her.

The snow was falling harder as I made my way to her apartment. With Ava occupying her, I had time. I'd yet to venture into her apartment, but after hearing her confession, the thought of stepping into her private space had me so turned on I couldn't resist. Making a stop in the spare apartment first, I dusted the snow off, then removed my boots and coat so I wouldn't leave any trace of my presence.

The smell of Riley's perfume lingered in the air when I stepped into the apartment. I breathed it in, closing my eyes while arousal spread through my body, my dick pulsing in response. I moved through the studio slowly, letting my fingers linger on her possessions like doing so would bring me closer to her. All it did was give me a raging hard-on. The pair of lace underwear near her bed didn't help and as I fingered it, the temptation to bring it to my nose was strong. Reminding myself that I'd have the real thing soon enough, I forced myself to focus. Touching her things wasn't my reason for being there. I was determined to find some clue as to why she was running, and there had to be something in her apartment to give me the answer. I'd had my men look when they delivered the new furniture, but they weren't always as thorough as I was. Riffling through every drawer and every box she had stored in the tiny closet, I found no trace of Mason or any part of Riley's past. It was like she'd left everything but her clothes and furniture behind.

Starting a new life.

The sound of her key in the door startled me. I hadn't given myself enough time, and I clenched my jaw, stepping into the closet, thankful she used it for storage since I'd bought her a larger wardrobe to hold her clothes. I held my breath, watching her through the cracked door as she tossed her clothes on the bed and walked through her apartment in her bra and thong. She was killing me, and I couldn't help picturing her walking around my house like that.

I could no longer see her, but I heard her hum an off-key tune, the sound bringing a smile to my face. After a few minutes, she came back into view, stretching and removing her bra. The sight of her made my cock so hard that I worried she'd hear it throbbing against my pants. Her breasts jiggled as she walked across the room and took a tank top from her bed. Knowing how dirty this was, how depraved it was to be spying on her this close only helped to intensify the discomfort in my pants.

She settled in the bed, sitting with her legs crossed as she gnawed at her bottom lip. I was so close to her, hidden only a few steps away, and the thrill of it was addictive.

"Fuck, Riley," she muttered. "You're obsessed."

She flopped back on the bed, running her hands over her chest before she said, "Stupid. There's no way that's even close to the real thing."

I knew she was talking about me, and the thought sent my pulse racing. I had every desire to step from the closet and give her the real thing. To fuck her like I wanted and make her mine. Gripping my fists, I forced myself to calm down. Leaving the closet while she was awake would only frighten her. I needed to remain in control, no matter that I now knew she wanted me as desperately as I wanted her. Knowing only moved the game to the next level. She'd be easier to reel in now because she wouldn't hesitate. I could have her, and I hadn't even had to work hard for her. But I still wanted to play, to tease her until she was so needy she'd bend to my will and shatter completely.

Her hand lingered on her breast, and my breath caught. I watched, enraptured as she touched herself. She worked her shirt up, her breasts exposed in the dim of the fairy lights that were strung along her ceiling. Her breasts were perfect, and I couldn't wait to feel them. The clouds hid the moon, but there was enough light for me to see every inch of the skin I was longing to touch. Her feet twisted as her fingers pushed below her panties, her sigh seeping through the quiet room.

My heart was pounding so hard, my cock straining to break free, and when she muttered a feral, "fuck me," shoving her panties all the way off, I reached into my pants and grabbed it. Her legs spread wide as her fingers disappeared, a moan lighting the air, her back arching in a beautiful curve. I stroked my throbbing dick, biting back the growl as she grew closer, my own quiet movements bringing me to the edge. I was gripping the wall so hard, my nails tore into the paint.

She drew her knee up as she cried out and I lost it, coming with her, my release spilling into my pants and shirt as I forced back my groan, holding my panting breaths in while the ecstasy poured through me. My legs were shaking so badly I didn't know if I could remain standing.

Riley drew her hand from between her legs, and my eyes tried to focus while my body calmed. Her leg twisted as if a residual aftershock had gone through her, and she released a deep sigh. I let go of myself, cursing my lack of control and the mess I'd made.

I waited in silence for her to fall asleep so I could leave, my eyes remaining riveted to her body. She pulled her shirt down but didn't bother to put her panties back on before she pulled the comforter up, covering what I craved touching. I watched, my mind overcome with the idea that she'd fingered herself to thoughts of me again, that I'd been so close that I could smell her arousal, so close that I'd come with her. Her moves had destroyed every ounce of control I had, leaving me like a teenage boy watching porn. But this had been nothing like that—my body controlled by her moves, her moans, her climax calling mine forth.

Adjusting myself and ignoring the sticky mess in my clothes, I emerged from the closet once I saw she was in a deep sleep.

Unplugging the fairy lights in case she woke, I stepped closer to her, picking up her discarded panties and pocketing them. I eyed the scarves that draped over her headboard, pulling them off and imagining her tied up with them. Letting the soft silk drift through my fingers, I knew I had a choice. I could be a true bastard and use the scarves to take advantage of her. To finally have her and feel what it would be like to sink into the wetness I knew lay between her legs. My dick twitched, springing back to life. Or I could walk out and continue playing my game. I was a wicked man, but taking a woman against her will was where I drew the line. Even with as wrong as voyeuristically jerking off in her closet was, I wouldn't cross the line. I wanted her to be willing, to have her cries be welcome ones.

I leaned over, the smell of her arousal on her fingers tempting me to lick them. Ignoring the desire, I brushed her hair from her face. She stirred, and I knew my time was up. Leaning closer to her, I murmured, "Good girl," then draped the scarves over her eyes and walked away, rushing from the apartment just as I heard her confused mumbling.

Returning to the spare apartment, I glanced at the camera while cleaning myself up, removing my shirt and wiping away the cum that was sticking to me. Light from the lamp on Riley's side table highlighted her actions. She had pulled the blankets up tight around her as she gripped the scarves. A frightened look sat in her eyes, and they frantically searched the room before falling on the open closet door. Guilt trickled through my mind, guilt that I'd scared her. Fear was my game, everyone feared me, so why shouldn't she? But no matter how I tried to justify it, the guilt remained.

I sat, watching her tentatively step from the bed and search for the discarded panties that were now in my possession. She cursed and gave up, snatching a pair of tiny shorts from the end of her bed. Once she covered herself, she opened the closet door before checking the other parts of her apartment. I took the panties from my pocket, fingering the lace and contemplating whether sniffing them put me in a category I didn't want to be in. I'd just hidden in a woman's closet and watched her finger herself while I jerked off. I wasn't certain what criminal level that took me to, but considering murder was already on my rap sheet, that didn't concern me.

What concerned me was how close I'd come to giving into my craving for Riley. I didn't know if I'd ever craved a woman the way I now craved Riley Brinks. And that was a problem.

I sat at the edge of my bed, all the lights on. A man had been in my apartment. The thought terrified me. At first, I'd worried he'd found me. That I hadn't hidden far enough away, that somehow he'd discovered me. Clint Randall. The man who had opened my eyes to my brother's misdeeds in such a terrifying way that I'd been looking behind me since that night. Nightmares had plagued me for months, and even now, they occasionally returned. The man I'd given my heart to just to have him tear it from me and stomp all over it when he tried to kill me. A man who had infiltrated my brother's ranks then seduced me with his bad boy smile and tattooed biceps. He'd been everything I loved in a man, and I'd fallen like an idiot, naïve to Mason's secret life and the enemies he had. An enemy who had found me and used me until the day he turned on Mason by trying to kill me.

He'd gotten away from Mason's men that night as Mason had rushed me to the hospital. The wounds had healed, but the scars, both physical and emotional, hadn't. It had been the fracturing moment in my relationship with my brother. And as much as he told me he'd always protected me, keeping me blind to it all to keep me safe, it didn't matter.

I'd moved into his guesthouse at his insistence, and since Clint was still out there somewhere, I'd had no choice. Even now, Clint was still out there. Whether in hiding or hunting me, I didn't know. But in my mind, he was hunting me. So when I'd woken to the touch of fingers on my cheek and the hushed 'good girl', my first thought had been Clint. But the touch wasn't right. It was too gentle, and Clint had never been a gentle man. He'd insisted we keep our relationship from Mason, so when he took me, it was quick and dirty, his fingers forcing my orgasms from me. Clint wouldn't have stood by and watched me touch myself. He would have taken what he wanted, then strangled and beaten me. There would have been no gentle brushing of his fingers over my cheek and certainly no hushed words. If the scarves hadn't fallen over my eyes as they blinked open, I may have even thought I was dreaming. But it hadn't been a dream. The scarves gripped in my hand were proof of that. My heart was thudding so loudly, I could barely think.

Someone had been in my apartment. Someone who had watched as I'd touched myself while imagining Greyson Tides was fucking me hard. My cheeks warmed with the memory of my fantasy until I reminded myself that someone had watched from my closet. The door hadn't been wide open when I'd gone to sleep. Had he jerked off to the sight? The dirtiness of the thought gave me a strange stir of flutters in my lower belly.

"Shit, what is wrong with you, Riley?" I muttered, rising to check that he hadn't come in through the window.

I stopped in my tracks, realizing that the top lock on my door was unlocked and I always locked it. The sight confirmed that someone had indeed been here. There was no sign that he'd broken the lock, and I clicked it back into place. Nothing but the scarves even looked touched. It was as if he'd only entered to watch me touch myself.

I sat back on the bed, my mind muddled. I should have reported it and called the police, but what would I tell them? Some guy snuck into my apartment and watched me finger fuck myself? It was too embarrassing to even confess. And he hadn't hurt me. He hadn't sexually assaulted me, which seemed strange. Why hadn't he touched me? He'd only brushed his fingers over my face delicately. I brought my hand to my cheek, remembering how the softness and the low words had stirred me. There was something familiar about the touch that I couldn't place, something soothing.

I decided not to report the incident, but promised myself I would call the landlord in the morning and have my locks changed. There was no plausible way for me to explain it to anyone and so I rationalized the incident before I snuggled at the end of my bed, staring at the scarves in my hand, wondering why there was a familiar scent in the air. It took me a while, my mind awake and actively going through the event, but eventually my eyes grew weary, and sleep took me.

Morning came too fast, and I was too on edge to think clearly. I trudged my way to the shower, wondering how I was going to make it through work when I couldn't get my mind from the touch of the stranger's fingers on my face. Or that he'd watched me come, some warped part of me wanting to believe he'd come with me, that he was some sexy morally gray guy like in the dark romances I read. In reality, I knew I should have been worried and more frightened, but it hadn't been Clint, and nothing frightened me like he did.

When I emerged from the bathroom, toweling my hair, I stopped in my tracks, my heart pounding. A beautiful bouquet of pink and white peonies sat on my counter. My favorite flower. The scarves lay delicately draped next to them. Drawing my eyes up, I scanned my apartment, checking under the bed and in the closet again. No one was there, but those flowers hadn't been there before I'd stepped into the shower. Tentatively, I picked up the note that sat nestled within them.

You came magnificently, like a good girl.

My thighs clenched, my hand shaking. He'd been here. My stranger. My stranger? I was losing it. This man had broken into my apartment twice now and I was calling him mine? Clint must have damaged me completely, because this was not normal. I dropped the note, backing from the flowers, my mind a confused jumble of thoughts, my body a convoluted mix of excitement. I sat on the loveseat, staring at the flowers. They were lovely and delicate.

My phone sat on the table across from them and I rose, ready to pick it up and call the building manager, to have someone change the locks, but I sat back down. This was dangerous, and if my brother weren't a killer and feared mob boss, if Clint hadn't exposed me to violence and pain, I would have been terrified. But I wasn't. Sure, this man had left me shaken, but I was also curious. Why go to the trouble of coming back and bringing me flowers? It seemed such a sweet gesture for the creepy act the night before. Why not rape me and never return? Something about the gentle touch to my cheek, the 'good girl' on the air, the note, and the flowers gave me pause. It was almost endearing, like something a lover would do. And maybe I was just so messed up that I was looking for a good guy in every man I came in contact with because so many had hurt me.

I bit my lip, worrying about my sanity and wishing I had someone to talk to. I didn't know Ava enough to trust her with this and the only friend I had was the sister of Mason's best friend. I couldn't take the chance that she'd tell Tyson who would tell Mason.

Thinking of Mason brought a melancholy ache to my chest. A part of me wanted to hear his voice, to have him talk some sense into me. Rising, I reached into my purse, pulling out my second phone. The one I had yet to use because I knew it would bring

Mason to my door. I placed it on the table, not turning it on. Sitting, I pulled my knees to my chest, looking between the phone and the flowers. Instinct told me to call, to have him come get me, to tell him what was going on because he would rescue me and pull me out of this warped sense of normalcy I was giving to someone who was clearly stalking me enough to know my favorite flower.

I dropped my head to my knees. I didn't want to be rescued. I didn't even know if I needed to be rescued. Someone was playing a game with me, but it wasn't one that was hurting me. It was teasing me, twisting my sense of normalcy, and letting me accept that this was okay. And I didn't know what to think of that. Chewing my lip, I glanced at my bed, where I'd slept with the scarves in my hand. A reminder of my stranger. And in return for watching me, he'd brought me flowers.

"Dammit, Riley," I muttered. "This is wrong."

I grabbed both phones, throwing my everyday one in my purse and tucking the other in the back pocket of my jeans before throwing on my boots and coat. Leaving, I rushed to the parking garage where I stored my car, forgetting that my hair was still wet until the winter air hit my face. It was too late now; I wasn't turning back because the need to hear my brother's voice was driving me. He had always been the calm, controlled one who made things better, even if I hadn't seen who he really was.

While I wanted to hear Mason's voice, I still wanted to remain free of his control. There was no way I could call him from my apartment, or he'd discover where I was. Leaving the parking garage, I headed west, only stopping to get gas and coffee once I left the city.

I wasn't one to make friends easily. Ava was an exception, but I wasn't about to tell her anything about my past. I rarely let anyone that close to me. I had acquaintances, but no one from home who I could call. Anyone else I knew was too close to

Mason. And in reality, I only had Mason. He was my best friend. We'd always been close. Even though he was nine years older, he'd never pushed me away. I'd run in his pack, hung with him and Tyson, and stayed in their circle. I saw now that he'd placed me there on purpose. Needing me close to keep watch over me, to dictate all the pieces of my life without knowing. Pretending I had autonomy while keeping me on a short leash. A leash I'd rebelled against when Clint had tempted me. Clint was the first time I'd lied to my brother, the first time I'd ever gone behind his back. But it hadn't been the first time he'd lied to me.

I drove all morning. I wanted to be far from Bridgeville, far from the life I was creating for myself. A life free of my brother's reign.

By noon, I pulled into a mall in Creekwood. It was far enough from Bridgeville that Mason wouldn't connect the two. I did some shopping to ensure I'd be on the cameras and grabbed some lunch. When I'd procrastinated enough, I returned to my car and powered the phone, seeing the picture of me and Mason load on my lock screen. The sight caused a sob to rip from me. As much as I hated my brother for what he'd done, I loved him. I wasn't sure what I was going to say, but I needed to hear his voice.

With a shaking finger, I hit his name and waited for him to answer. He picked up immediately.

"Riley?" His voice was a mix of anger and worry.

"Hi, Mason."

"Where the fuck are you? Do you have any idea how worried I've been? Are you safe?"

"I'm fine."

"Fine? You left without a note, without a goodbye. Cleaned your storage unit out in the middle of the night? That's not fine! What the fuck are you doing, Ri?"

I held the phone back as he screamed at me.

"Come home now."

"I'm not coming home," I answered, his anger shifting my mood. What had I thought? That he wouldn't yell at me for hurting him? Because I knew that's what I'd done. Hurt him because he'd hurt me.

"What the fuck do you mean, you're not coming home? I will find you and drag your ass back to Treemont."

"No, you won't, Mace. You'll leave me be. I can't live under your shadow anymore. What you did—"

"What I did? What did I do, Riley? Tell me. Because all I've ever done is keep you safe. You were the one who snuck behind my back and who let that asshole in."

"An asshole I would have known about if you'd ever bothered to tell me the truth!"

He was quiet. I couldn't tell if he was seething or contemplating my words.

"Just come home, Ri. Please." His voice was softer, and it squeezed at my heart.

I held the phone to my chest, trying not to cry. I wanted to run to him. To tell him what was happening and have him guide me. Bringing the phone back, I bit back my tears.

"No. I need to do this on my own, Mace. You need to let me go. I don't belong in your world, and you don't want me in it...or you would have let me in long ago."

"Riley—"

I disconnected, powering the phone back down and sliding down the side of the car. The tears rushed out like a torrent. It hurt to hear his voice, hurt to bring him pain, and I wrestled with that. I wiped my eyes, pushing the tears away and rose, climbing into my car and making the journey back to Bridgeville. By the time I made it to my apartment, it was dark, and I was exhausted. I ordered delivery but didn't bother eating it. Curling into bed, I finally drifted to sleep with the salt of my tears still dried on my cheeks.

There was no sign of my stranger that night, but when I woke, the smell of coffee invaded my senses. He'd brought me breakfast. A cup of my favorite coffee, exactly like I ordered it, and a bagel sat on my table, my scarves laid out next to them. I couldn't help smiling. The act was sweet, even if it was creepy to know someone had been in my apartment again, watching me sleep. If he'd wanted to hurt me, he would have that first night.

I decided I'd continue the game with my stranger. He was giving me something to think about other than Greyson Tides, the pain of missing Mason, and the ever-looming threat of Clint Randall.

I SPENT SUNDAY ALONE, contemplating my dilemma, my rising obsession with Greyson Tides, and the growing curiosity with my stranger. The scarves I'd found over my eyes that night twisted in my hand as I absently held them. My eyes remained fixed on my bedframe with its slatted boards, perfectly distanced. The racing of my heart was a worrying reaction to the thought that he hadn't haphazardly thrown the scarves over my eyes to give him time to leave. They'd been deliberate, a calculated move. One he'd considered yet turned from. He'd wanted to touch me, to do more than watch me, more than brush his fingers over my cheek.

The pounding in my chest was loud. He'd moved the scarves both mornings, an invitation to play, a seeking of permission to go further. My hands shook at the mere fact that I was thinking of playing his game. It had been a long time since anyone had touched me, aside from the brief temptation of Greyson in the elevator.

I rested my head in my palm, the soft material of the scarves pressing against my skin. My stomach flipped in excitement. I attracted bad boys, and they drew me in. This wasn't the worst one I'd had, but this would be right up there under Clint. An invitation for the stranger who'd been stalking me the past few days, likely more, to take what he wanted.

"Shit, Riley, you've gone mad," I scolded myself. But my insides twisted in anticipation.

I needed to get out, to take my mind off this, but I didn't know where to go. Ava was working a double at the bar, so I couldn't talk to her unless I left my apartment. And maybe that's what I needed to do. Dropping the scarves, I changed, throwing on a pair of jeans and a sweater. I ran my fingers through my hair and put a light layer of makeup on before heading out.

The bar was just down the street and as I walked, I wondered if my stranger was following me. The thought, although creepy, gave me some comfort. It was dark, and I didn't like being out this late by myself. Clint was a shadow ever looming over me, one that was hard to escape, and I pulled my coat closer, hurrying my steps. I found Ava behind the bar, serving drinks. The place was bustling for a Sunday night.

"Riley!" she yelled, rushing over to where I'd squeezed in at the bar. Her hair was piled in two small, tight buns that gave her a girlish look. "What can I get you? And why are you out this late?"

"It's not that late. It's only eight o'clock!" I argued before ordering a beer.

She ran off to get me one, helping a few customers on the way back. A handsome man with a boyish grin shoved his way in next to me, but Ava plopped the beer in front of me and gave him a look. "Don't even think about it, Paul. You're not messing with this one."

"Still sore you weren't a keeper, Ava?" he asked, flashing an even bigger grin.

"Nah, just that you don't know how to make a girl come, even with as much as you fuck."

His grin faltered, and he huffed off.

"What was that about?" I asked.

"He pestered me until I gave in. He's pretty to look at and that body is definitely worth the fuck, but he's a prick, a player you want to avoid." She hopped away to pour a few more drinks before she grabbed someone to cover for her and returned to me. "I can point out the good ones if you're looking for someone to warm your bed, though."

I thought about her offer. Was that what I wanted? Why I'd gone out in the first place? To have someone fuck the thoughts of my stranger from my mind, to make me come so hard Greyson Tides would disappear for at least a few hours? Two men who wouldn't leave my mind, neither of whom I should have let in there in the first place.

"Nah, I just wanted to get out."

She gave me a questioning look. "Everything okay?"

How did I tell her I was missing my brother? That I was homesick, being stalked, and considering inviting my stalker into my life to take my mind from an unhealthy obsession with Greyson Tides? I couldn't, so I nodded and took a drink. "I just wanted to say hi and see what nightlife here was like."

"You don't strike me as a nightlife girl. You're more of a homebody," she teased. "Do you ever do anything impulsive?"

"I came here," I groused.

She nudged me with her elbow and continued chatting. But her words played in my head. I'd never been the impulsive type, although Mason would have argued my taste in men was impulsive. And maybe that was why, by the time I left the bar, I had decided to tempt fate with my stranger, to take a chance and see what happened.

Once I prepared for bed, I laid the scarves out on my table with a note that my trembling hands placed in the center.

Tie me up, touch me, taste me, but nothing more.
My safe word is 'yet'.

Sleep eluded me for a few hours, but I finally drifted off.

When I woke without the touch of my stranger, the disappointment was unhealthy, but it dissipated when I found the answer to my invitation waiting beside a fresh cup of coffee and a chocolate chip muffin. One small word that sent my heart racing.

Tonight.

GREYSON

Riley had made an unexpected move in my game. With each passing day, I was finding Riley to be anything but predictable, like I'd first thought. She hadn't reported the incident, hadn't even called the building manager to have her locks changed. No, she'd let me continue playing.

She'd left town on Sunday, the act leaving me baffled. The flowers I'd left for her had given her a mixed reaction, and I could see her battling with her need to like them and hate them. I'd watched as she pulled out a phone and sat it on her table, staring blankly at it. It wasn't the one she used daily, which had me curious. But then she left, running to her car and driving off. I couldn't follow, but I had a tracker on her phone, so I'd waited all morning, my nerves fraught that she was so far from me. I could see that she'd stopped in Creekwood, but not where or why. It had killed me knowing she wasn't close.

But then she'd returned, as if she hadn't been gone all day. I'd left her another gift, her reaction still not what I'd expected. I'd almost lost it when she left her apartment, walking the dark streets by herself, but when she'd gone into the bar, I was livid. Stuck outside, waiting in the shadows for her, visions of other men hitting on her had consumed me. My rage and envy had grown with every passing minute. Den had buzzed my phone multiple times, scolding me for leaving my men on edge the entire time. They had strict orders to keep their distance when I was watching Riley, and even stricter orders to keep their mouths shut about it.

The experience had left me so out of control, so aching to rush in there after her, that I'd considered stopping my game. This wasn't necessary; I had her where I wanted her. She would easily spread her legs for me, but patience was what set me apart from everyone else and something that had earned me my reputation. I didn't rush in. I took my time, making my enemies squirm, watching their nerves grow. Waiting days, months, sometimes even years before enacting my revenge. But when I struck, I struck hard.

I wouldn't rush this, and I would play with Riley, continue stalking her, coming into her life faceless and unknown until I broke her, and I would continue taunting her in everyday life, until she was so desperate for me that she was begging. I'd have her both ways, vulnerable and nervous, obedient and wanting.

But the invitation she'd left me last night had almost knocked me over. I knew she had a side to her that was more than she showed; she was Mason's sister. But I was beginning to see that it was a side that made her even more tempting to me.

Tie me up, touch me, taste me.

The words resounded through my head as I watched her get ready for bed. I was finding it hard to be patient with how sexy and inviting she looked. Her tank top reached just to where her tiny panties sat. She had her legs crossed and in her hand she held the black silk blindfold I'd left her to find when she returned home from work. The note that accompanied it was still on her kitchen table—*I'll follow your bidding, but you obey my one rule. Wear this and don't remove it.*

The scarves were on her bedside table, loose and ready for what I had in mind and from her placement of them, exactly what she had in mind. My desire flared thinking of it, the anticipation of seeing her place the blindfold, killing me. The tightness in my fists was extreme when she brought it to her eyes and tied it. Her movements had me mesmerized and so enraptured that my cock nearly jumped through my pants.

I remained hidden in the apartment next door until she laid down and the signs of sleep finally revealed themselves. Patiently, I waited longer, hearing Ava come down the hall at two, then giving it another good thirty minutes before I made my way to Riley's. Slipping my key in her door, I tried to calm the rapid beating of my heart. I stood in the dim lighting, listening to her soft breathing, before I stepped closer to her. She'd kicked the blankets off, her shirt riding up her stomach, her bare skin calling to me. I reached for the scarves, then delicately touched her, waiting to see if she'd wake. When she didn't, I guided her wrist up, tying a scarf around it and weaving it through the slats in the headboard before doing the same with her other wrist.

Shit, I couldn't believe I was doing this, but I needed to touch her, and it was the ideal time to torment her. Torment seemed an odd word for the pleasure I was about to give her. I lowered her panties, hissing as I dragged them over her ankles and she moaned, her legs spreading beautifully for me. My heart was pounding frantically with anticipation. I was almost salivating, my need to taste her was so great. There was something dangerously naughty about this, something almost wrong until I reminded myself that she'd given me permission. She had dictated the rules, and I planned to follow them, but that didn't mean I wouldn't enjoy every minute.

When she still hadn't woken, I secured her ankles, then slid between her legs, pushing her thighs further apart and hearing her breathing change. The light was too low to see any details, but her fragrance was intoxicating. I sank my tongue into her, her moan loud as I stifled mine. Slipping my finger into her, I tongued her clit, trying my best to ignore the urge to just take her. It was strong, but I wouldn't cross the line she'd drawn. This was about pleasuring her. I'd fuck her when she was willing, and I was sure from our interaction in the elevator and the way she'd breathed my name in her sleep that it wouldn't be long before I had my cock buried in her.

She twitched, and I heard her gasp as she woke, freezing momentarily as if she'd forgotten our arrangement.

"Shhh, baby girl," I mumbled against her skin to muffle my voice. "Just say the word and I'll stop."

I flicked my tongue over her clit.

"What's the word?" she asked in a raspy voice that made my balls ache.

"Yet. Now be a good girl and come for me."

Her groan was deep, and I sank my tongue back into her.

"But you're supposed to be a bad guy," she moaned.

"I'm the baddest there is, but I won't take what you don't offer. I will, however, rip that climax from you." Tired of disguising my voice and needing to taste her more, I pushed my finger deep into her and sucked her clit, her body lurching as she threw her head back.

She relaxed, her legs quivering beautifully. I smoothed my hand up her stomach, the tremble of her muscles reminding me that my own nerves threatened to betray the controlled demeanor I was exuding. Murder, deception, and torture were things that came naturally to me, but stalking, and whatever this was, was new. Something I would never have done with anyone, but Riley had me so out of sorts, my craving for her so intense that I needed this taste of her, or my control would break and my game would end. I pushed her shirt up, caressing her breast, her nipple firming at my touch. This was torture; my dick was throbbing so badly I thought it might rip through my pants to get to her. She smelled as delectable as she tasted and I glided my tongue up her stomach, feeling another quiver of her muscles tinged with nerves. Purposely, I kept myself above her, not touching my body to hers, my hands and mouth all I would allow myself for fear of not being able to uphold her request if I pressed against her skin.

Drawing my tongue around her nipple, I cupped her breast, hearing her long sigh and the shake within it. The sound was like a siren's call that I was finding hard to resist. I dragged my teeth along her nipple, her sigh morphing to a deep moan that set my body on fire.

"Fuck," I muttered, my voice so hoarse I knew she wouldn't recognize it. She tensed, a quiet whimper falling from her lip. It was a sound that I wanted to hear repeatedly, and it nestled into my consciousness, fixing its claws in me like a mark of ownership I didn't understand.

Dropping back down between her legs, I gripped her thighs, needing to feel her come undone for me and knowing I needed to be quick, no matter how I wanted to make this last, otherwise, I'd lose control and ravage her the way my cock was urging me to.

I flicked my tongue against her clit, her back arching beautifully. Her thighs quivered again as I slid my finger back into her and pushed my tongue over her clit. I couldn't get enough of the way they trembled and the power my every move seemed to have over her body. She lifted slightly, my finger sinking further and eliciting a low moan from her. Shit, she was about to destroy me. I kept my finger there, wishing it were me filling her instead. My craving for her had peaked, and I was one moan away from giving up my game. Bringing it back out, I brushed my thumb over her clit and sank my tongue back into her, trying to restrain my groan as her thighs pushed against me. Her loud cry lit an inferno in me, and I fought the urge to free my cock and fuck her. But this wasn't about me, and I'd made her a promise. I didn't want to hurt her or frighten her by breaking that promise, no matter how much this was hurting me. When that change in my mentality had occurred, I wasn't sure. I should have been inducing fear and not moans. I shouldn't have cared if I was hurting her or frightening her. That had been my intent from the start. But this had turned into something more. This was now about her and the pleasure I wanted to bring her. I was about to tear the climax from her, and the thought was enough to make me lose it. I drove two fingers into her, taunting her clit with my tongue and twisting my fingers just right so that I hit a spot that tore a raw cry from her. She pushed against my face as she broke, her body convulsing around me.

She was glorious, and I licked until she was whimpering. Giving her one last flick against her clit, I lifted myself, resisting the urge to free my cock and thrust it into her.

"Good girl, that was beautiful," I murmured, licking my fingers loud enough for her to hear before loosening her one hand. I turned and walked out, knowing she wouldn't see me in the dark and that I'd be out of sight by the time she freed herself.

Returning to the spare apartment, I dropped to my seat, licking my fingers again and stroking my raging hard-on through my pants. My body was shaking with excitement, my cock painfully rebelling because I hadn't satisfied it with the beauty whose body had writhed to my touch. Riley was still lying on the bed, her breathing hard. I could see the rise and fall of her chest, and the weakened state I'd left her in. After a few minutes, she untied herself and removed the mask. The bliss on her face was intense enough for me to see even as far as she was from the camera. Not bothering to put her underwear back on, she pulled the blankets up and snuggled under them, her smile lighting the room.

I sat there for a long time, calming myself and regaining my control. Tonight had been a stepping point, and now that I'd tasted her, I knew there was no turning back.

Standing at my office window, I watched Riley make her way up the street. She had pulled her ebony hair into a tight ponytail, but the wind still fought to free it, just like my fingers wanted to do. I'd upped my game, enjoying her smile a little too much when I left her my small gifts. She was so beautiful when she was unguarded that it almost hurt to look at her. The need I had for her had grown to an obsessive craving, one I was having difficulty controlling now that I'd handed her the power and let her dictate the next move. Tasting her had almost destroyed me. I could still feel her coming against my mouth, taste her essence, smell her fragrance, and it was driving me mad. I wanted more, and that need rebelled against my need for control. This was my game, one I was slowly losing.

As I lost sight of Riley, my phone buzzed.

"Speak," I said.

"I found out where she went," Alec said. I'd tasked him with finding the mystery of her disappearance over the weekend.

"Where."

"She stopped in a mall. Cameras show her shopping and eating lunch."

"That's it? All the stores we have in the city, and she drove hours away to Creekwood. There must be something else. Did she meet someone?" Envy gripped me and I clenched my jaw.

"No, she was alone. I pulled footage from the parking lot, though. She made a phone call. It wasn't long, but whoever she spoke to, it was emotional. It looked like she was crying before she got in the car and left."

That was confounding and the idea that she was in pain bothered me on an entirely irrational level.

"Thanks, Alec. Let me know if you find anything more."

"I did."

Smirking, I said, "Of course you did. That's why I keep you around. What did you find?"

"Our guy on Brinks reported he took a heated phone call that same day around the same time as Riley was in Creekwood. He was on site with one of his developers when he stopped the conversation short and took a call. He was screaming into his phone at whoever was on the other end, and by the time he finished, he looked upset. Called the meeting off and stormed away. His men moved out immediately."

"Let me guess. They went to Creekwood?" I asked, wondering what exactly had gone down between Riley and her brother. I hadn't started keeping tabs on him until she arrived in town. I needed to know if he was stepping foot in my city.

"Exactly."

What the fuck was going on? There was something I was missing, and it was driving me mad.

"Anything more?"

"No, that's all I found out."

"You did good, Alec. Keep your men on Mason and let me know if he moves again."

"Will do, boss."

There was more to Riley Brinks than I thought, and I was ready to discover her secrets.

I walked to my desk and paged Sherry. "Send Miss Brinks up."

Waiting patiently as I looked out at the snow, I thought through my options. I wanted the game to move to the next level, but a part of me wanted to continue seeing her unguarded smiles, to play with her secretly like I had the prior night. That meant I needed patience. I wanted my control back, however, and now was the time to take it back. I wasn't ready to give her everything, but I was ready to play more.

I heard her slowly open the door. "You wanted to see me?" she asked in that seductive drawl that made my balls tighten.

"Sit, Miss Brinks." I continued staring at the street but could hear that she'd chosen to sit in the seat in front of my desk. "On the desk."

She made a slight noise similar to a cry, and I could sense her confusion. I still didn't turn to her yet, needing to maintain my control. I wanted her on edge and keeping my back to her ensured she would be.

"Did I not make myself clear?"

"I...no...I mean, yes, you did."

I smiled at her uncertainty and listened as she rose and sat on my desk before I turned. The breath fled me like it did every time I looked at her. Her hair was still windblown. Strands sat loose around her temple and her neck, and I had the urge to walk over and wrap one around my finger. To feel the softness of it.

Walking over to her, I stepped into her space, smelling the subtle scent of her perfume. Her green eyes were wide with anticipation. Her skirt had slipped up, exposing more of her thigh, and I studied her reaction as I stepped closer and rested my hand on it. Her lips parted, her breaths growing shorter as I smoothed my hand along her skin.

"There's a rule I have for my employees, Miss Brinks."

"Yes," she said rather breathlessly.

"No dating."

She scrunched her brows, her eyes dipping to my fingers, which were pushing her skirt higher. I loved how she wore no stockings below her boots, even in the cold, but I was curious what she'd look like with a sexy pair of thigh highs and a garter.

"Does that rule not extend to you?" she asked, meeting my eyes.

Lifting my hand, I tipped her chin, brushing my finger down her neck. "No."

She inhaled so sharply I could see it pained her.

"There are no rules or laws that extend to me, Miss Brinks. I do what I want because I can. And I get what I want because I can."

"And what do you want?" Her eyes were lush, the green deep with desire, and I fought not to kiss her.

"I want you to keep away from Matt."

She creased her eyes, drawing back from me.

"Matt?"

"Yes," I said, stepping back and loving the disappointment in her eyes.

"I haven't done anything with Matt."

"No? That's not the rumor that came from his mouth." She looked like I'd slapped her. I'd heard the talk from the bastard's mouth once she turned him down. No one was close enough to her to tell her the truth, so instead they were talking about it behind her back. I should have fired them all. Should have killed the fucker and made him suffer horribly before putting him out of his misery. He'd pay, but I would use his stupidity as leverage.

"What rumor?" There was that guarded look again.

"That he fucked you the night he walked you home."

Her mouth dropped, and her reaction stung me. "I didn't sleep with him."

I crossed my arms as she rose from the desk, the skirt falling to cover that delicate skin.

"I swear, I didn't. I turned him down when he asked me out." She chewed her lip, and I could see her emotion changing. "That asshole. I'll kick his balls so hard he won't be able to fuck anyone ever again."

I choked back my laugh. She was a spitfire, and I loved it. I'd only seen her fragile side, but I knew she'd run from Mason and that took nerve. She'd also invited me to play with her, letting her hunter in to taunt his prey, so she wasn't some frail flower.

I walked over to her, getting so close that she stepped back, the desk pinning her. Memories of her cry of ecstasy returned and the way her body had writhed below my touch, making it almost hard to keep up my charade. I reached out and picked up one of the loose strands of her hair, curling it in my finger like I'd imagined. "So you didn't sleep with him?"

"No," she murmured, her anger fading.

"Good. Are you sleeping with anyone else?"

A faint blush started on her cheeks, and I knew exactly why it was there. She remained quiet, and I tipped her chin back up to me. "Answer the question, Miss Brinks. Are you fucking anyone else?"

"Why does it matter?" she dared. "Why is that any of your business?"

I stepped against her, relishing the feel of her body pressing against mine. She exhaled wonderfully, and I slid my hand down her arm.

Leaning close to her ear, I said, "Because you are mine, Riley Brinks. And no other man will touch you."

She shuddered, her body arching into mine, and I wanted to keep her there, to touch every inch of her and have her come undone for me. But this was a game...one I was failing at miserably. I stepped from her and turned my back, walking to my window.

"I'll see that Matt packs his things today. That's all. Miss Brinks."

She didn't leave and I could feel her eyes on me.

"That's all?"

I glanced over at her. "Did I not make myself clear?"

"I...fuck. What if I..."

I turned to her, seeing the look in her eyes. The same one she'd given me in the elevator and on the street. Longing. She wanted me, but the way I was going about this bothered her sense of rightness. Her mystery lover confounded the situation for her because now she had two men she wanted, and I'd just laid claim to her.

"If what?"

She held her head higher. "What if I don't want to be yours?"

I clenched my jaw, feeling my eyes harden. "Is there someone else I need to worry about, Miss Brinks?"

She stammered before saying, "Riley. It's Riley. What if there is?"

I fought my need to grin because I knew exactly who that was, and I knew I'd be paying her a visit tonight to taste a little more of my girl. I strode to her, grasping her by the back of the neck and loving the sigh she released. "Then I'll kill him for daring to touch what's mine."

Her mouth fell open, and I could feel the tremble of her nerves. "You can't kill someone," she said meekly.

"For you, I would, Riley. For you, I would burn down the world."

Releasing her, I walked to my desk and grabbed my coat. She continued to stand there, speechless.

"Go back to work, Miss Brinks."

I strode past her, leaving her there, and made my way from the building. My body was ablaze with my need for her, but I wasn't ready to act on it yet. I would, however, play tonight. I'd staked my claim, and now it was time to let her know who owned her.

I don't know how long I stood in Greyson Tides' office. His words played through my mind. I was his. It was such an arrogant and assumptive thing to say. To think I was an object to be taken and owned by him. I didn't even know him. But I wanted him. Shit, I wanted him so badly I was aching. Yet all he'd done was give me words. He'd barely touched me.

I brushed the strand of hair he'd touched away from my cheek and huffed from the office, not bothering to give his assistant a goodbye. Folding my arms as the elevator took me back to the main floor, I tried to figure out why I wanted this man so intensely. Why I'd wanted him to lift my skirt the rest of the way and fuck me right on his desk.

Because he was a bad boy. I'd known it from the moment I found out who he was, which was strange because the man who'd helped me on the street my first day hadn't given me that impression. It was almost like that had been an unguarded version of him.

"Riley," Ken's voice interrupted my thoughts.

He gestured for me to join him in his office. I closed the door and sat, still discombobulated from my interaction with Greyson.

"Matt no longer works for us. I've removed him from the building. I'm sorry for what he did."

"You knew?" I asked, glancing around and wondering who else in the office had heard his lies.

"I was the one who reported the incident to Greyson. I overheard it in the lunchroom and put a stop to the rumors."

"It wasn't true," I said quickly, irritated that my new colleagues now thought I was the office slut. No wonder they'd distanced themselves.

"I know, which is why I brought it to Greyson rather than just shutting down Matt's talk. I've addressed it with the rest of the staff."

I could feel the tension in my neck. "That's just great," I muttered.

"Listen. Don't let this experience bias you against the team. They're good people. Matt's been on probation for other incidents, and this was the last straw. Greyson seems interested in seeing you succeed, so don't let this bother you."

I knew exactly why he was interested in seeing me succeed: he'd put some unrequited claim on me.

"The company Christmas party is in a few days. He insists you attend so we can make it up to you."

Raising a brow, I sat up. "I don't do Christmas parties."

I'd heard the others talking about the lavish annual Christmas party Greyson Tides threw for his employees and the more influential people in town. I wanted nothing to do with the holiday festivities. This was my first year away from Mason, and I knew it would be melancholy. I'd left him right before Thanksgiving and even that had hurt. We usually spent that weekend decorating the house and putting the tree up. The thought threatened to drown me.

"Riley?"

I looked back up at Ken. "Sorry. I guess I'm just still upset by this Matt thing. I don't think I can do a Christmas party."

I stood, needing to get away.

"Think about it. If Greyson says you're going, trust me, there's no way you'll avoid it. Why don't you take the rest of the day off? Get away and clear your head."

I nodded and left, gathering my things and logging off for the day. I was a jumble of thoughts and emotions. Anger at Matt for his asshole move, shock at Greyson's words and even more so at my acceptance of them, and sadness from thoughts of missing Christmas with Mason.

I walked around the city, planting myself on a park bench and staring off into space until it grew too cold. Reluctantly, I trudged home, which offered another set of confused thoughts —the uninvited guest who had turned into an invited one. What he'd done to me had been undeniably erotic. I'd never come so hard, and I'd never had a man dedicate all his attention to my climax. And, oh, how I'd climaxed. Just the thought of it had my thighs shaking. His touch had been ecstasy. Everything about it was wrong, but now that he'd given me a taste of what he could do, I craved more. Almost as much as I craved Greyson Tides.

Greyson's hand on my thigh, his words of ownership sent a warmth flooding between my legs. I chewed my lip, thinking how familiar that touch had been, how the scent of his cologne had lingered on his skin with a strange familiarity.

Pausing at my door, I grasped for the thought that was forming in my mind but lingering just beyond reach. With a shrug, I let the thought go and opened the door, my heart thudding as I spotted the beautiful bracelet that was lying atop the blindfold. My stranger had left me another gift, a row of emeralds and diamonds that sparkled in the light. Another gift. An expensive gift. Before, they'd been simple—flowers, coffee, small things that told me little about him other than he knew my tastes. The blindfold that had left me quivering with anticipation, fear blended with excitement.

But this… I picked up the bracelet. This was the gift of a man who had money, a confident man who was making a statement.

My mind was stringing pieces together, grasping for the one to solidify the thought that was forming.

"Whoa, that is one nice piece of jewelry." I jumped, dropping the bracelet at Ava's voice. "Now I'm convinced you have a sugar daddy, and you won't convince me otherwise."

Turning to her, I shook my head in denial, seeing that I'd been so distracted by my thoughts that I'd left the door open.

"I don't know what I have," I mumbled.

She lifted a brow, one I saw now had a hoop through it.

"That's new," I noted, pointing to it.

She shrugged. "I enjoy adding piercings and tats every now and then. I'm not sure I like this one, but I'm giving it a test run."

There were times I envied Ava. She was so free-spirited, braver than I saw myself. Mason would have called her reckless, but I admired her ability to be who she was without worrying about the constraints that held me back. I'd never even gotten a tattoo, and considering how many my brother had, that was saying something.

"It's cute," I said, retrieving the bracelet from where it had fallen and returning it to the table. "But I like the stud in your nose better."

"Yeah, that one's my favorite."

I turned back to her. "You have more than those two…and your ears?" I tried not to gape at her, but it was hard not to, especially when she said, "The clit was painful but so worth it."

My eyes grew so wide, I swear I looked like a cartoon character. Ava laughed hard enough that she had to hold on to the door.

"I love shocking you, Riley. You're so easy."

"So, you don't have one?"

"Oh, I definitely have one and the guys love it. But then, I prefer it when they have piercings, too."

The thought made my cheeks burn because, as much as I loved a bad boy, I'd never been with one who'd braved that.

"All right, you need to share details," I said.

"Done. How about we order takeout and watch a movie at my place?"

The tension slid from my shoulders and with a relieved sigh, I said, "Sounds perfect."

I didn't want to be in my apartment, the reminders of my stranger were too prominent. And I didn't want to be alone with memories of Greyson's touch on my skin, either.

"Let me get changed and I'll be down in a few." I kicked my shoes off but before she left, I stopped her, saying, "And I want you to tell me what you know about the Christmas party Greyson Tides throws every year."

Now it was time for her eyes to go wide. "Oh, I forgot about that! You're one of his employees, so you get to go!" Her excitement was palpable, and she looked about to jump up and down.

"I don't think I will. Christmas parties aren't really my thing."

"Are you kidding me? I hate those things, too, but I'd die for a chance to go to that one. It's always the talk of the town. He spares no expense and each year the theme is different. They throw it in that fancy hotel we passed when we were shopping. You know, the one that looks like it costs a fortune to stay at."

I remembered that hotel. It was extravagant and looked like someplace Mason would have picked to stay. There was a red carpet leading to the doors and two well-dressed doormen in uniform. I could only imagine what the inside looked like. Mason had taken me to an island resort when I was younger. His best friend, Tyson, had gone with us. Tyson was like my second big brother, and he was a player. He'd hooked up with women most of the trip, leaving me and Mason to joke about his flavor of the day. The hotel where we'd stayed was breathtaking and had a pool that overlooked the ocean, workers who catered to your every need, and everything set up to perfection. It had been a wonderful trip that was now tarnished by the knowledge that Mason owned the resort. Yet another lie that had surfaced when the truth came out.

The hotel Ava and I had passed by reminded me of that resort. For a moment, my mind wondered if the rooms were just as beautiful, the beds soft and plush enough to surround me as Greyson's body pushed me into it.

Shaking my head to free the image from my mind, I said, "I don't know. Apparently I'm expected to go but..." How did I tell her I would be a mess without Mason the closer the holidays came, or that I was craving Greyson Tides like my body craved food, or that I was having a bizarre affair with a stranger who snuck into my room at night and tongued me until I fell apart. "I'll probably stay home."

"You're insane," she grumbled. "Get changed and get your ass down to my apartment so I can talk you into going. No one in their right mind would miss that party."

She was still complaining about my decision as the door shut behind her. My eyes fell back to the bracelet, and I picked it up, my fingers lingering on the beautiful gems. Maybe I needed to go, if anything, just to break the routine that was setting in and the complacency that was building around a situation that should have had me worried.

Changing quickly, I grabbed a bottle of wine and headed down the hall to Ava's determined to leave my thoughts of Greyson Tides, my stranger, and soul shattering orgasms behind.

MY STRANGER DIDN'T RETURN the next two nights and if he hadn't surprised me each morning with coffee and a treat, I would have been worried. It didn't seem normal that a stranger who regularly broke into my apartment could make me happy, but he did, and with each passing day, a part of me missed his touch. This morning, another bracelet appeared, this one not as flashy. A simple silver chain with tiny pink and white peony charms attached to it. I'd worn it to work, fingering the tiny flowers and wondering where he was and who he was. The nagging thoughts in the back of my mind kept telling me I was missing something, but every time I tried to focus on it, I encountered an interruption.

Ready to kick my heels off and snuggle in for the night, I unlocked my door. My stomach knotted, and I bit my lip to hold back the excited cry. The blindfold sat on my table in the middle of the scarves. Alongside it was a container of takeout soup from the local deli. Ignoring the soup, I picked up the note.

Wear this and nothing else.

My heart thumped uncontrollably, and I chewed my lip, wondering if heeding his request would give him the okay for more. I didn't know that I wanted more. Something about that seemed wrong.

"Shit, Riley. Everything about this seems wrong," I muttered.

I dropped the blindfold and picked up the soup, my mind whirring. I wanted to feel his touch again, but anything more seemed like too much. Changing into my sleeping shirt and a pair of shorts, I scrolled through the news on my phone, ignoring the blindfold and my jumble of confused thoughts while I slurped my soup.

When it was too late to ignore it any longer, I picked up the blindfold, running my hands along the smooth material before removing my clothes and crawling into bed. Curling under the blankets, I took a deep breath and tied it around my eyes like I had the first time. As my stomach clenched with nerves, I laid down and waited, the anticipation building with each passing minute. But nothing happened. The door didn't open, no one emerged from the closet, and eventually, I grew too tired to avoid sleep's call.

The touch of hands startled me awake as my wrists dug painfully into the scarves now tied to my headboard. I let out a small cry. He was back, and I trembled with anticipation.

"No screaming, baby girl, unless you're coming." His words tore a moan from me, his voice low and muffled, but no less sexy.

His hand skirted along my body, the comforter no longer covering my nudity. My stomach quivered, my knee drawing up when his thumb slipped through my arousal. The hitch of my breath caused him to chuckle against my stomach, a reaction that seemed like a comfortable one shared between two lovers rather than what we were.

"My safe word and rules are still in force," I mumbled through my moan.

"Of course they are," he said, his mouth on my calf, making his voice hard to distinguish.

I relaxed, his fingers plunging into me at the same moment. My back arched with the sensations that gripped me. He'd left my legs free this time, and I drew my knee higher.

As he moved up my body, his stubble tickled my stomach and his hardness pressed into me. I avoided pushing into it like I wanted to. He had hovered over me the first night, but now it was firm against me and ready for me to yield. But I wasn't ready to cross that line, and Greyson Tides' words hummed through my head. I was his and no one would touch me. Yet, this man was touching me. He was sucking on my breast, ripping a cry from me as he rubbed my other nipple between his fingers. He flicked his tongue over my nipple then dragged his hands down my body, which quivered at his touch. That touch was firm but gentle and so different from what I was used to that I melted into it just as I had the first time. Every inch of me was on fire, his touch bringing me closer to breaking with every passing second. He dragged his mouth over my stomach, then between my legs until his tongue was against my clit. Another moan fell from my lips, his fingers rubbing through my arousal, then plunging into me. My body responded, pleasure bounding through me in ripples. I cried out, wishing it was his cock and wanting him to fuck me, knowing it was wrong but wanting it anyway and resisting my desire to beg him to take me. With each lick, my need for more rose, my climax teetering on the edge until he twisted his finger, and I came undone, my body clenching down around his fingers, my thighs pushing at his shoulders. My cry was intense, ripped from a part of me I'd hidden away with the trauma and pain of the last few months.

"That's a good girl," he mumbled, his voice hoarse.

His touch left me, and there was an emptiness that shouldn't have been there. The scarf loosened, and as I freed myself, I debated bringing the blindfold up, liking the suspense of not knowing. When I finally lifted it, he was gone, and I flopped my head back, not bothering to untie myself. He'd left me spent, depleted, and satisfied without satisfying himself once again. It seemed like a good guy thing to do, yet he clearly wasn't one...just like Greyson Tides. It was bad enough that Greyson had me infatuated. Now I had my stranger. Two men who had crossed the line in different ways. Two men who were owning me in ways I didn't want to admit.

The last two days had been excruciating. With my obsession so out of control, I'd convinced myself to keep my distance from Riley. As much as I'd wanted to indulge in her, I needed her to crave me as achingly as I craved her. So I'd bided my time, avoiding the office and working from my home instead, making the rounds with Den to check in on my businesses. By the morning of the third day, I could no longer contain myself, vowing I'd play with her and indulge my fantasies some more. The Christmas party I threw for my employees and associates was in a few more days and that was when I'd make my big move, letting her tell me how much she wanted me and fucking her like I craved, without a blindfold, without sneaking in. This time, she would invite me back, if I could wait long enough to make it to her apartment, if I didn't take her against the wall right there in the middle of the party. She wanted me enough. I'd sensed it in my office, and she might just be as needy as I was, needy enough to wrap her legs around me as I pounded her into the wall of the closest empty room.

But for now, I was playing my part as her unseen suitor,

leaving her gifts and relishing the feel of her coming against my mouth. She'd fallen apart so hard, her cry was still resounding through my ears. It was a sound that would stay with me forever. One I wanted to hear repeatedly for the rest of my life.

I stared at the camera as she went back to sleep, my dick too hard to keep from stroking myself. She'd accepted my offer, waiting naked for me, the sight riveting me when I watched her crawl into bed. My cock was still throbbing from the experience, and I cursed my weakness, pulling it free and letting my hands replicate the way I imagined her muscles would bear down on me, the way they had on my fingers. With every thought of her body, the taste of her, the feel of her clenching down around my fingers, my motion quickened until my release hit me, ricocheting through my body. Cum climbed up my stomach, my groan filling the quiet room. I closed my eyes, Riley still on my mind as my body finally quieted.

I'd wanted to break my resolve and fuck her, but she'd stated her rules again and I'd honored them. Some part of me suspected she'd welcome it even with her protests, but I wouldn't test that suspicion, no matter how much I wanted it. It was better this way. There was no way I could hide my identity if I was buried to the hilt inside of her. I needed to be patient.

My plan was moving into the next stage, but that plan had morphed. I was in too deep, and I couldn't find my way back out. I'd almost lost control with her in my office. That fucker Matt had dared boast that he'd slept with her. I knew he hadn't, but that hadn't stopped the talk around the office. I'd paid him a visit, ensuring he knew never to step foot in my city again and warning him that if he went anywhere near her again, he wouldn't live to spread rumors about it. I had Den escort him out of my city once I'd left him too bruised and bloodied to protest.

No one took what was mine. And Riley was mine.

Cursing myself for my weakness, I cleaned up and left, hating the distance it put between us. I wanted her now like I'd never wanted anything, and nothing would stop me from having her. I spent a sleepless night with Riley on my mind, rising early enough to slip a small gift and a cup of coffee into her apartment before she woke. Standing over her, I watched the peaceful rise and fall of her breathing, noticing how she still clutched the blindfold in her hand. The way my heart beat at the sight had me worrying that I'd fallen deeper than I'd intended.

I kept my distance from her for the next few days, leaving small tokens for her each morning. The emerald bracelet I'd left her was on her wrist when I stood hidden in the shadows as she walked into the building. This evening was the Christmas party, the night I planned to fully claim her, to let her know I'd had her this entire time. I didn't go into the office after her, instead I had my men drive me to her apartment where I had one last gift to give her. I draped the blue dress I'd bought Riley on the table in her apartment, tucking a note in the stilettos I'd chosen for her. Buying women's clothes wasn't my usual thing, but I wanted her to look just right when I finally took her. Before heading out, I placed the shoes and a diamond necklace on the dress.

I had a meeting out-of-town, and it had me on edge. I didn't like leaving Riley. Something about how she had run from Treemont still bothered me. I knew she was running from her brother, but instinct told me there was more to it. Mason was still hunting for her, which was part of the reason I was leaving town. He'd asked for a meeting on neutral grounds, his tone serious. And I knew if he asked to meet me, something concerning was on his mind.

His men were still scouring for his rogue henchman, Clint Randall, and suspicion told me this meeting had something to do with him. I took Den and Tinge with me, letting Den drive. Another car followed with two more of my men, armed and ready if Mason pulled anything. Like Den, Tinge was a beast of a man, all muscle and loyal to a fault. All my men were loyal, which made me question what had happened with Mason's man. He'd been at this for fewer years than I had, but he was still experienced enough to vet anyone on his team. It was the nature of the business.

My knuckles cracked as I stepped from the car, ensuring my jacket was far enough back to show my gun. Mason wasn't stupid. I didn't think he'd attempt anything. We were enemies, but there was an unspoken rule, one he'd crossed when he'd dared venture into my territory. He'd retreated, but it had left me planning my vengeance, something Riley had walked right into. Although I wasn't so sure my plan was going how I'd intended because the thought of devastating her now was wrenching.

"Grey," Mason said, a bit too cocky for my taste. His green eyes reminded me of his sister's. The same black hair fell in waves over his forehead.

"I don't count you among my friends, Brinks, and not even my friends call me Grey."

"Do you have any friends, Grey...son?"

He was a smartass and my need to teach him a lesson reared back to the forefront.

"Why did you ask me to meet you? I can't imagine any reason you would have to reach out to me."

His bravado faltered, and I saw the worry behind it. He was too sharp. There was no way he would mention Riley's disappearance. She was an asset to anyone who found her. A wild card, an advantage that could weaken or even destroy him, which was precisely how I'd planned to use her. And exactly why I didn't like being so far from her.

"I have a man who's gone rogue. He needs to be put down, but he's gone underground," he admitted.

So, that's what this was about. Clint Randall. "Must have done something serious to have you asking me for a favor."

He narrowed his eyes, and I could see the way he was gritting his teeth at having to admit that was exactly what he was doing.

"It doesn't matter. But it's serious, and he's a threat. His name is Clint Randall. Has he surfaced in Bridgeville?"

Time to get some answers. "What did he do, Brinks?"

He clenched his jaw, his eyes darkening. "He damaged something of mine."

That had been an unexpected answer.

"What?" I pushed, needing the details. Something bothering Mason Brinks enough to go to this extreme was serious. "If he's that big of a threat, I need to know what might be lurking in my city."

The muscles in his jaw stood out as he gripped his fists. "He hurt my sister."

I had to hide my reaction because his answer was one I hadn't expected. No wonder Mason was hunting him.

"Tell me how and I might help you."

"What the fuck do you need to know for?" he snapped.

"Your emotions are your weakness, Mason. You may want to work on that. Now tell me what the fuck this Clint Randall did to your sister to have Mason Brinks this worked up."

"Let's just say he used her and put her in the hospital."

I couldn't stop my hiss and he narrowed his eyes.

"No wonder you're hot," I said, recovering. "If someone did that to my sister, I'd want him dead, too."

"You have a sister?"

"No, but I wouldn't tell you, even if I did. What's in it for me if I help you?"

Rolling his neck, he remained quiet. I could see he didn't want to give me anything, but I didn't do things for free.

Tyson walked closer to us, and I sensed Den do the same, both men ready to attack if either Mason or I made a wrong move.

"What do you want in exchange?" Mason asked, his teeth gritted.

And there was my opening, a way to finally get the brat under my control. He really was desperate, and I imagined this wouldn't be happening if Riley was under his watch. But with her on the run, he had no choice.

I folded my arms over my chest. "You fall in line, continue to stay in your territory, but if I need your assistance, you don't blink. I bark, you jump from now on."

He narrowed his eyes, and Tyson flexed his muscles.

"Don't pull that shit, Raines," I said to Tyson. "You two are asking me to use my resources to fix your problem," I growled.

"If I agree, it goes both ways," Mason said after a few moments of contemplation.

"A truce between our sides?" It was an interesting prospect, but I needed him under my control and not the other way.

"Yes."

"Only under my lead, always my lead," I said, loving the tick in his jaw.

"You want me to give control to you, Tides? Are you shitting me? I would never do that."

I didn't bother responding. Instead, I turned my back on them and walked to the car, Den following.

"Fuck you, Tides. Fine, but conditionally!" He was losing control and having him begging was almost as rewarding as having his sister come against my mouth. I hid the smile that thought caused and turned.

Mason was scowling like the pouting brat he was. "Conditionally?" I asked. "I don't do conditionally. Let's try this, Brinks. You fall in line and stay out of my territory. I'll do the same, but you will fall in line behind me. You align with me, and we become the combined force of the province. It will ensure the others keep their noses out of our business and won't dare try to move against either of us."

He studied me. Mason was an intelligent man. I'd watched how quickly he'd risen to his position, gathering resources and power that had taken me years to gain. Until he finally took down the family that had run his city for decades. That kind of skill came naturally to him, just as it did to me, only I had been at this a lot longer than he had.

"Deal," he said. "But if you cross me, Tides, I won't hesitate to take you down."

It was an empty threat. I held the true power in the province, and everyone knew it. "You weren't successful the first time, so I'd keep that bravado in check or I'll let your little problem fester."

The muscles in his jaw were so tight it looked like they might pop.

"I'll need everything you have on Randall. And I mean everything," I demanded.

Tyson walked to the car and returned with a folder. I took it from him, flipping through the details and pictures. Clint Randall looked like trouble. He was nothing but muscle. His tattoos covered every inch of his arms and extended up his neck. His brown eyes held only contempt, and I wondered how Mason hadn't seen past the sneer that screamed distrustful ass to me. I spotted the marking on his bicep and brought the picture closer to study it.

"You let a Bad Omen in your ranks?" The Bad Omen were a family I'd run out of Bridgeville twenty years earlier. They worked underground, infiltrating other families and taking them down from the inside. They were notorious and those of us who'd been around when they first formed knew what to look for. Mason didn't.

He snatched the picture from me.

"The tattoo on his left bicep," I explained.

"Fuck," he grumbled before he shoved it back to me.

"So he got in and almost took you down. Didn't think I'd see the day another family would take you down, Mason." It was a compliment laced with an insult and he knew it.

"He didn't take me down."

"No, he didn't succeed, but he almost did." I flipped through, looking for anything on Riley. "I need to know exactly what he did to your sister." I didn't need it to find Randall, but I needed to know.

"What the fuck do you need to know that for?" Tyson barked. "You want my help?"

"You don't need to know those details," Mason said.

"Then I don't need to help you. If you let a Bad Omen escape and there's a chance he's in Bridgeville, I can easily turn that into a reason to turn on you, Brinks. Now tell me what the fuck he did to your sister."

I didn't play and my enemies knew it. That was one reason I was the most feared boss of the provinces. I didn't hesitate to kill if anything threatened my business or my people.

"He manipulated her," Tyson said, running a hand through his mop of brown hair. He seemed just as upset as Mason, and I wondered how close he and Riley were. Close enough to have slept with her? I looked between the two men, but they didn't seem like that mistake had ever come between them.

Mason shot him a look.

"What Mace? He wants to know. Why not tell him?" He glanced back at me. "Seduced her—"

"Fucked her?" A stab of envy jolted through me at the thought.

Mason growled.

"Wow, you really dropped your guard, didn't you, Brinks?"

"Fuck off, Tides."

"So your rat fucked your sister and used her to hurt you, hoping it would weaken you."

"He didn't weaken me. I found the prick." He was gripping his hands so tight the veins in his arms were raised. "Found where he had her and..."

The emotion surfaced, and I knew the asshole had hurt Riley enough that there were scars. "Found her?" I asked, thinking back on her reaction when she'd first seen the furniture I'd given her. The fear in her eyes, the tears as she'd sat and cried.

"He had her sneak around behind our back," Tyson said. "Kept it secret until he was ready to strike. Lured her out of town and held her hostage. He turned on her, then on us. We found her..." He looked over at Mason, who nodded for him to continue. "Bruised and bloodied. He used her as a shield so we couldn't kill him."

My anger was rising as I tried to keep my reaction from showing. He'd done what I'd set out to do. Exactly what I'd wanted to do—manipulate her and throw her back at her brother to weaken him, then kill them both. Only I'd become distracted, my plan taking a backseat to what Riley did to me.

"He stabbed her and in trying to save her, we lost him," Mason finished for him.

"Smart man," I said, hiding the vile hatred I had for Clint Randall. Mason may not have killed him, but I would, and I would make him suffer for daring to lay a finger on Riley.

"Consider him dead," I said, loosening my hold on the folder, which had ripped from the pressure I had on it. I turned away and walked back to my car. "I'll send you his body when I've suitably tortured him."

I didn't look back, signaling for Den to drive off. I couldn't have stayed or said anything more because the anger was spilling over.

"Fuck!" The dashboard buckled from the force of my punch.

Den stayed quiet, and I stared at the file for the rest of the trip, angry at the fucker who'd hurt Riley. Angry at myself for not knowing, for doing the same things he'd done and causing her more fear, more pain. I'd stalked her, broken in, tied her up... although she'd given me consent, trusting that I wouldn't hurt her for reasons I still didn't completely understand.

Regardless, I'd brought up memories she was running from, and I hated myself for it. Hated that I had intended to do exactly what I now regretted because I was falling for Riley Brinks. And that was a place I had never expected to be, one that made me vulnerable, one that left me confused. I was tired of the game because I wanted Riley Brinks to be mine completely. That way, I could protect her and keep Clint Randall from ever touching her again. Mason may have failed at keeping her safe, but I wouldn't.

Chapter Fourteen

I hadn't seen Greyson Tides in days. I searched for him every time I entered the office, glanced through the lobby, or made an excuse to get coffee from the client coffee bar to catch a glimpse of him walking through to his elevator. He'd left me disappointed each time, as had my stranger. After that last night of pleasure, he hadn't returned. His gifts continued, however, surprising me every morning.

Returning to my apartment, I absently fingered the more extravagant bracelet he'd left me. It was beautiful. The emeralds in it matched my eyes, and I wondered if he'd chosen it for that reason. If he had, it meant he had seen my eyes in the daylight. I shrugged away the disturbing sense that thought brought to me, rationalizing it just as I did the fact that this man somehow gained access to my apartment daily without me knowing. The word stalker tried to seep into my consciousness, but I was too far into the fairy tale I'd told myself this was to give it any notion.

It was likely good that I hadn't seen Greyson. The claim he'd laid on me in his office still tingled through my veins, the feel of his hand on my skin still as prominent as my stranger's touch. When he made his next move on me, I'd have to reconcile the need I had for my mystery man with the one I had for Greyson. I fingered the bracelet again, pushing the worry away and smiling as I walked into my apartment, my eyes falling on the beautiful dress draped over my table. The Christmas party was tonight. I'd said I wasn't going, but Sherry had visited me before leaving the office and reminded me that Greyson expected me. Her words had sent a jolt of currents soaring through me. Greyson Tides wanted me there, and I had no doubt he'd make his next move, whatever that might be.

I closed the door and moved to the table, fingering the satin navy dress. It was so delicate, something that seemed foreign to my life now. I ran a finger over the sparkly silver shoes that sat upon it, noting the designer brand label. There was a note tucked in one and I picked it up.

I expect a dance with you tonight.

My stranger. He'd left me the dress and would be at the party this evening. I shivered in anticipation, my mind going through all the possibilities of finally finding out who he was. And of having both him and Greyson in one room. I didn't know what to expect from that situation. Greyson had staked his claim, but my stranger had his own claim on me. Sure, it was one that was built on a very sketchy foundation, but it was one I couldn't deny.

A necklace lay on the dress, the diamonds shimmering, and I absently touched them. Diamonds? Emeralds? Dresses that looked like they cost a fortune? My stranger had money, and that thought stirred something in my mind along with the other nudges that had flitted in and out of my thoughts the past week. There was something I was missing—the scent that lingered in the air, the firm and familiar touch, the lavish gifts.

I glanced around the apartment at the expensive furnishings Greyson had given me. I knew the difference between luxury brands and bargain brands. Mason had been my guardian long enough, and everything he bought me was high-end. Greyson Tides had money at his disposal, time on his hands, and a smirk that burned through me like the tongue of my stranger on my skin.

I rushed to my cabinets, pulling open the drawer where I kept every note the stranger had left me. And the note from Greyson. Holding tight to the newest note, I held Greyson's up to it, inhaling sharply as I saw the similarities.

Dropping the notes, I backed up. Greyson Tides was my stranger. I should have seen it earlier, never understanding how my stranger could enter my apartment and forgetting that Greyson had decorated it while I wasn't there. He had to have a key. My stranger had never broken in. There was never a sign of forced entry. That was why his touch was familiar and the scent that filled my senses when he came to me. It was Greyson all along.

I sat on my bed, trying to reconcile the fact that both men who infatuated me were the same man. Greyson had been the one to bring me to ecstasy each time. His touch was the one I was craving every night. Chewing my lip, I looked back at the dress. He was playing a game, and I wondered why he'd gone to so much trouble. Maybe he just had strange fetishes...but he'd stated I was his in his office. Claiming me. I thought of the way he'd lifted my skirt, his hand running up my thigh, and how familiar his touch was. It had been a blatant show of power, a sign he expected I wouldn't see. All this time, he'd been toying with me, letting me crave him while taking a taste of me. Watching me, knowing my every like and dislike. I thought of the first time I'd met him, thinking it was a coincidence. It hadn't been. He'd been following me even that early, claiming his stake on me that first day.

Standing, I picked up the dress. If Greyson wanted to play a game, it was time to play along with him. I should have been angry, but everything about this situation went against my rational thoughts. Greyson Tides went against them. I'd wanted him from the moment his blue eyes met mine. I'd wanted him when he'd claimed I was his and that he'd kill anyone who touched me. I'd wanted him when he had me tied up and writhing against his tongue. I still wanted him, but this time, I wanted him on my terms, and I wanted all of him. The game was about to become mine.

I took my time getting ready, thinking through my plan as I did. The dress fit perfectly. It flowed to cover my feet, leaving just the sparkly tips of the stilettos showing. The back dipped dangerously low, and I was glad my breasts were small because I couldn't wear a bra. I could have used something for support, but Greyson had started a game I intended to play. Seeing his reaction to my free breasts seemed like something worth risking. I piled my hair up in an elegant bun, leaving long wisps free. I looked like a princess from a fairy tale...my fairy tale. If only I could show Ava... shit, wait until she found out Greyson Tides wanted me. I hadn't told her about my stranger. I wasn't sure how she would react, and the fact that I'd continued to let him play was warped beyond any understanding I could attribute to anyone hearing the story.

If Greyson desired me, he was going to have me. And after tonight, if I had my way, he'd have me completely because when I was through, I would own Greyson as much as he wanted to own me.

I WAS MATTING my lip gloss when my phone buzzed.

Greyson Tides.

Damn, how had he put his number in my phone? And how had I not noticed? The message simply said a car was waiting for me. A car? He'd even sent a car for me. I rummaged through my closet for something pretty to cover my shoulders from the cold. I had nothing that would work, but my scarves caught my eye. Their extra-long length had made them perfect for tying me up, an act that juxtaposed the memory and delicate beauty of them.

They'd now come to represent a forbidden affair, one that toed the line of criminal only because I had invited it. To anyone else, it would be grounds for prison time. But I wasn't anyone else, and neither was Greyson Tides. Shrugging, I grabbed them and layered them before draping them elegantly around my shoulders. They hung the perfect length down the front of the dress, as any other wrap would. I touched the top one, noting how the rich red hue complimented the blue in the dress. My heart beat at the overt sign, and I wondered if he'd play along or if my boldness would make him step back. He didn't strike me as the type of man to back away so easily from a game he'd brazenly started, one he'd determined he'd already won.

Giving myself a last glance in the mirror, I rushed from the apartment and down to the black sedan that was waiting on the curb. The driver nodded to me and opened the door. I felt like a princess on her way to the ball. He'd even cleared a path in the snow so my shoes wouldn't get wet. As I settled into the seat, I wondered if that had been Greyson's instructions or just a thoughtful gesture from the driver.

I rested my head against the seat, my stomach a bundle of nerves. Thoughts of Greyson and everything he'd done since I first arrived filled my head. From saving my purse to decorating my apartment to sneaking in my apartment and pleasuring me. Anger should have been the emotion I was feeling, but he'd done nothing to hurt me. I knew hurt. I knew betrayal. I knew fear. And nothing he'd done had brought me any of those emotions. Once I trusted that he wouldn't hurt me, I'd invited him to touch me. I'd invited him into my life.

The hotel was on the upper end of town, near the shopping district. It stood tall and regal, warm light spilling from its doors as my driver helped me from the car. The doormen held the doors open for me while I walked up the red carpet, feeling like a movie star.

Blue and white snowflakes adorned the pillars in the lobby

and the staircase that led to the second floor, where the ballroom was. I held my breath as I climbed, my nerves tingling through me like butterflies on a spring day. Just like the night I'd fled Treemont, there was no turning back now. I was in charge, and this was my game now, no matter what Greyson Tides expected.

Music streamed from the ballroom, a pale bluish light adding to the ambiance as I took my first steps in. I couldn't stop myself from gaping, my eyes taking in everything down to the tiniest of details. I'd been to a few parties Mason had hosted, but none were as extravagant as this. Tables sat throughout the room with vibrant blue and white roses. A chandelier with too many crystals to count hung above a dance floor, sending sparkles of light out that looked like snowflakes in the blue haze of the room. Frosted garland and twinkling lights hung from the ceiling. Royal blue cloth with tiny snowflakes embroidered into it covered each table. White tea lights in long glass cylinders sat in the center, surrounded by more roses, these white with blue frosted petals.

I could have looked in wonder the entire night had my focus not settled on Greyson. He was standing in the far corner, resting against the wall with his arms crossed. It was clear he didn't want to socialize. This was for his guests and not for him. I wondered if he bothered to attend every year or if he was only there for me. The thought sent a cascade of tremors through me. He lifted his blue eyes to me, a sexy curve forming on his lips. He looked even yummier than he usually did. His auburn hair was dark in the lighting, making his blue eyes even more startling. The tux he wore fit perfectly and left me hungry with the way it emphasized his toned figure. My heart stammered, and I hated the effect he had on me. How easily he unraveled me with just the intensity of his gaze.

My path didn't falter. I avoided the stares and the murmurs as I walked through the tables and stopped halfway on the dance floor. It was time for me to take control of whatever game Greyson was playing. I raised a brow at him and parted my lips, seeing how his gaze faltered for just that moment. People continued to dance as the music slowed and Greyson left his place on the wall. His eyes didn't leave mine, and I knew we'd be the talk of the city in the morning. That I'd likely no longer have a job because Greyson Tides was the company's owner, and I was in a position under him. I didn't care. I wanted Greyson, and I knew he wanted me. He'd already laid his claim on me. He'd ripped orgasms from me that were more powerful than any I'd had and ingrained the touch of his hands on my skin as well as the pressure of his tongue on my clit.

"Miss Brinks," he said, stopping just shy of me. There was something sweet about the adoration that sat in his eyes, and it warmed my heart.

"Are you going to dance with me, Mr. Tides?" I asked. "Or is that inappropriate?"

He wrapped his arm around my waist and pulled me close, taking my hand in his. It felt natural, like he was meant to hold me, our hands fitting perfectly together.

"Like how you staked your claim on me?" I whispered.

He gave me a coy grin. "You look delectable, Miss Brinks. Maybe I'm paying you too much." He fingered the bracelet. "Or is there another man I need to worry about?" he said against my ear. He drew back, his eyes dark. "I think I told you what I thought about anyone touching you."

My insides quivered, warmth flowing between my legs. "Then I suppose you'll need to fight for me...Greyson."

His eyes searched mine and I could read the humor in them. He didn't know that I suspected, and he liked the game he was playing. I couldn't wait to take his power and stake my own claim.

He leaned close to my ear again, "I told you, Riley. I will burn this city, this province, this world down around you before I let anyone touch what's mine."

I couldn't stop my sharp inhale, his words weakening me to my core.

The music stopped, but he didn't let me go, even as another song started. His gaze was intense, and he seemed to see deep into my soul.

I leaned closer to him, letting my lips graze his neck, and murmured, "Then burn it down."

His eyes danced with hunger, melting me with their ferocity. For a moment, I almost forgot about the game and where we were. His hand slid up my back, the touch on my bare skin firm and confident. My body rebelled, the dampness between my legs growing and, as if he knew, his lips turned to a coy grin that had me teetering in my heels. I needed to move before I lost control of the game and gave in to my need for him. We were in a hotel. There were plenty of places for him to tear my dress off and take me like I was craving. And if I didn't make my move, that's exactly where he'd have me.

"It's time to finish laying your claim on me and no safe word will stop you this time, Mr. Tides," I said, backing out of his hold and feeling how his hand twitched like he wanted to keep me there.

I let my wrap slip, and he caught it as it fell. His eyes took in the scarves before he glanced back at me. The smile he gave me was mischievous, and it left my knees weak.

I turned and left him there with the scarves. I'd played my cards; now, I would wait to see if he would fold to me.

Chapter Fifteen

GREYSON

My eyes trailed Riley as she left the hotel. She was breathtaking, and I'd wanted nothing more than to steal her away and take the dress from her body one inch at a time. I had thought I wanted her before, but now that she'd turned my game on me, I was hooked. She'd figured it out. Of course she had. She was calculating like her brother.

Running my fingers along the silk scarves, I smiled at the overt act of wearing them tonight. It was a sign, an invitation, an acknowledgement that she accepted my claim on her, that she wanted to play my game.

Her words thundered through my mind. *Then burn it down.* The feel of her lips on my neck left me harder than her words had. I was more than ready to follow her out, to carry her to a room in the hotel and mark her as mine. But my games had never been about anything but control and I would make her wait.

I bided my time, making a few more required greetings before I left the hotel. This time, I didn't bother hiding my car or my men. I didn't give a fuck who saw me parked outside her apartment building. She wouldn't be working for me in the morning because she would be mine completely—no safe words, no rules, no limitations.

I wasn't a nervous person, but nerves were tingling through my stomach in anticipation of what was waiting for me. Passing the adjacent apartment, I went straight to hers, slipping my key into the lock and opening the door. The lights were out, but the moonlight streaming through her window highlighted her silhouette. She was lying on the bed, her blindfold on. The dress that clung to her perfect curves remained on, and she had her arms stretched above her head and ready to be tied. My cock twitched at the sight.

I rolled the scarves between my fingers, taking two and leaving the others aside. Sliding my hand along her arm, I stretched it out and loosely tied the scarf around it. As I walked the length of the bed, I let my fingers drift along her body, hearing her sigh and feeling her nerves quiver. I tied her other wrist to the first, then took my suit jacket off before undoing my tie and kicking off my shoes. I could see the trembles that continued as she waited in expectation. Unbuttoning my sleeves, I rolled them up before climbing on the bed, taking her leg in my hands and running my mouth along it as I pushed her dress up. When I reached her hips, I groaned. No panties stopped my path, and I continued until my hands cupped her breasts. I'd feasted on those breasts the last time I'd tasted her, and I was finding there was no part of Riley Brinks that I didn't want to feast upon. Her stomach quivered as I ran my tongue over it. My path continued until my cock was pressing against her warmth, straining to be set free so she could take it.

Circling her nipple with my tongue, I ran my hands up her neck, following its curve until my fingers threaded in her hair. I kissed her neck, tasting the berry lotion she wore and making my way to her mouth where I hovered over her lips, watching as they parted for me and grinning as she moaned my name.

"Tell me how you want me, baby girl," I said, not bothering to disguise my voice this time.

She shivered, and my cock grew even harder.

"Take me, Greyson."

"How, Riley?" I wanted to hear her say that she wanted me to fill her, to hear the consent and know she accepted that she was mine, that I now owned her.

"Fuck me."

I growled, my cock jumping as she pressed her pelvis into me.

"Who owns you, Riley?"

"You do, Greyson."

"Good girl." I didn't wait to remove my pants or to untie her. I dropped my hand, sliding my fingers through her wetness before unhooking my pants and freeing myself. I brought her leg up and set my tip against her clit, hearing her purr. I'd never wanted a woman as badly as I wanted Riley and when I sank into her, it was rapture. My groan was loud, and she lurched into me, straining against the scarves. Her legs wrapped around me, her heels digging further into me with each thrust. I sat back, running my hand along her body and tearing her dress from the slit up, exposing her to me entirely as she complained.

"I'll buy you another one," I said, kissing her.

Her lips were as soft as I'd imagined, her mouth sweet like morning dew, and my heart swelled. I kissed her like she was the last woman alive because I'd craved her for so long. She was the only woman I'd ever kissed this passionately, and I knew she was the only one I wanted to ever kiss again. Her body bent into mine as I slid my hand down her curves, touching her the way I'd desired, the way I'd dreamed, without the hindrance of clothing or hidden identities.

I was craving her touch, to experience the feel of her hands on me. I drew back, seeing the scarves digging into her wrists as she tried to reach for me. Grabbing my pocket knife from my pants, I clicked it open. Her breath caught, her body tensing.

Kissing her neck, I murmured, "I won't hurt you, Riley."

I reached up, and she bucked. "Don't," she cried, and I

stopped, the plea in her voice giving me pause. What had the asshole done to her? "They were my mother's. Please."

Her explanation reassured me, and I threw the knife to the side, reaching up and untying her wrist instead. Her body calmed, her arm coming around to touch me as I untied her other wrist. Slowly, I lifted her blindfold, seeing how her green eyes shimmered in the moonlight. They searched mine, her fingers coming to trace my jaw before they dropped to my chest. Hastily, she dug at my buttons until she pushed my shirt from me.

Weaving her fingers through my hair, she pulled my mouth to hers, kissing me as hungrily as I'd kissed her. Her feet pushed at my pants, and I couldn't contain the chuckle at the neediness of her moves. I continued moving in her, too enraptured by her warmth to stop. Even as my pants fell and her legs wrapped tight around my back again, I didn't stop my thrusts. I couldn't. I'd waited too long to feel her and it had been worth every minute I'd waited.

Dropping my mouth to her neck, I ran my hand over her body, taking the moment to still myself and slip my fingers between us. I teased her clit, pushing deeper into her at the same time that I dropped my mouth to her breast, sucking her nipple into my mouth and loving her groan. She pulled at my hair as she dug her heels further into me, and I could feel her tighten around my cock.

"Are you going to come for me like a good girl?" I said, taking her nipple between my teeth and pulling.

Her pelvis lurched into me, and she fell apart, her body convulsing around me. The feel of her muscles spasming around me was too much, and I moved my hands to hold her hips, driving into her as her head fell back with her cry. The sound destroyed me, my release hitting me like a storm while I gripped her waist, unable to control the climax that was tearing through me, shredding me to my core.

I dropped my head to her neck, waiting for the drowning

waves of my release to stop, yet never wanting them to end. When they finally ceased, I kissed her neck, relishing the way her fingers ran through my hair. I lifted my head, pushing myself to my elbows, and looked at her. A gleam of satisfaction twinkled in her sage eyes, and she gave me a coy smile.

"So," she began rather breathlessly. "I guess this means no gift in the morning?"

"I can think of a few gifts I could give you in the morning, Miss Brinks."

Her lips trembled before they parted perfectly.

"Unless you'd like me to sneak out like usual?" I asked.

She tilted her head, her eyes creasing. "Why the game, Greyson?"

I could have heard her say my name a thousand times and never grow tired of the sensation it gave me.

"Because I like to play with my prey before I move in for the kill. And you were delicious prey."

She drew in her breath, her eyes shifting.

"And am I still your prey?"

"Are you?" I asked, wanting to hear her say she was mine again.

Her fingers slid through my hair and down my face as if memorizing each contour.

"No," she said. "No more games, Greyson. Spend the night with me, fuck me again in the morning, and spend the day with me."

I lifted my brow. "Those are demands, Riley, and I don't like demands."

"I'm serious. I want you, and if you want to own me, no more games."

"No more games. But I may not wait until morning." I dropped my mouth to hers, taking her bottom lip between my teeth. "And I can promise you, it will be more than a day."

Her body lurched forward, and I caught it, pulling her to me and kissing her. It didn't take long before her touches had me ready to take her again, which I did well into the night, knowing this was just the beginning. Now that I'd made her mine, I planned to keep her. And I would crush anyone who stood in my way.

Stretching, I looked over to where I expected to find Greyson, but he wasn't there, and my heart dropped. My body was a blissful afterglow of what he'd done to me the night before. I rose and made my way to the bathroom, thinking of his touches, his kisses, the way he'd come with me. My stomach somersaulted at the thought.

I was still in a state of shock that he'd been my stranger all this time. That he'd been sneaking in, making me his prey, as he'd said. I wasn't sure what to make of the term. Given my past, it didn't settle well with me. That first time he'd come to me had terrified me. He didn't know the reason, but he had to have realized it would. And it made me curious as to why he'd chosen to come to me unseen each time, to play that kind of game. A game I had let him play because I'd trusted him after that first night for no better reason than the excitement of it.

Grabbing my robe, I padded into the kitchen, disappointed that Greyson wasn't there. I chewed my lip, wondering if he was done with me. If he'd played his game and caught his prey and would turn to someone else now that he'd conquered me. The thought caused a strange pang in my chest, one I didn't like.

I turned at the sound of a key in the door, my heart fluttering. Greyson entered, holding two cups of coffee. Snow highlighted his auburn hair and when he met my eyes, there was a sweet adoration to them, an unguarded moment that I suspected few saw. He smiled, that same wonderful smile he'd given me on the street my first day. The one that had reached in and captured my interest.

"Miss Brinks," he said slyly, his expression shifting.

"You know, Mr. Tides. Once your dick has made its way into me, I expect you to use my first name," I said playfully.

He placed the coffee on the table and removed his coat, shaking the snow from it before neatly laying it over a chair. That one move said so much about the man who had brought me to rapture and made me his.

"Should we talk about how and why you have a key to my apartment, Greyson?"

His blue eyes sparkled as he walked toward me. "Should we talk about why you have this on?" he asked, pushing the sleeve of my robe down. "And why you're out of bed?"

"You're deflecting my question."

"And you're not answering mine."

I gritted my teeth, which only encouraged him to slip his hand down and cup my breast as he kissed my neck. His skin was cold, and I shivered.

"I thought I told you I would ravage you again this morning."

My insides twisted with anticipation. No man I'd ever been with had made me come the way he had, had touched me the way he had. Each touch had seemed like he was worshipping me.

"You did," I sighed as he untied my robe. He threaded one hand through my hair and brought my lips to his as his other hand caressed its way down my body, sending goosebumps along my skin. I melted into him, hating that he broke my resolve, but loving what his touch did to me.

His kisses were sensual, not demanding or aggressive like the other men I'd been with.

"Greyson," I tried again.

"Riley."

He was infuriating, and he was breaking me again. He squeezed my ass, pushing me against his hardness, and my insides fluttered. I wanted him to take me again, but I wanted to talk, to have answers. He picked me up and sat me on the counter, draping his lips down my body. My thoughts fled, my head falling back as he spread my legs further and sank his tongue into me. So much for talking. I lost myself to the pleasure he was bringing me, his tongue summoning my release so that I fell apart, my body a surge of electrical currents that left me weak.

When he had unraveled me completely, he rose, wiping his mouth on the back of his hand and giving me a roguish smirk. I grabbed his shirt and jerked him to me, kissing him and feeling his surprise at the move as his smile grew against my lips.

"You wanted to talk, Riley?" he said between kisses.

"Talking can wait. Fuck me, Greyson." I needed to feel him inside of me again. Needed him to fill me, to take me to oblivion again, but this time to fall with me.

"We should work on that language of yours, Miss Brinks."

I worked his shirt free, pushing it from him and saying, "Fuck you, Mr. Tides."

He chuckled, and I knew then that the formalities would be part of our fun. There was something about the way he said my full name that reached in and owned me. And I wanted to be owned by Greyson Tides. No one else would ever own me the way he now did.

I fumbled with his pants, my hands hastily undoing them because I was craving him so desperately. As they tumbled to the floor, Greyson pulled me to him, sinking into me with a groan that lit every part of me on fire. He took me there, his touches needy as if being from me had left him hungry and I had to satisfy that hunger. He drew another climax from me, my body breaking in his arms as he continued to thrust into me, only then giving into his own rising release. As he came, he held me tight, his muscles shaking, his head dropping to the dip in my shoulder until his body relaxed.

Only when I lifted his head, forcing his eyes to mine, did he move. I traced his lips, wondering how this man had charmed his way into my heart and why I had let him.

"Don't hurt me, Greyson," I whispered. "Please, don't hurt me." It was a plea that came from the deepest recesses of my soul, because after what Clint had done to me, I'd promised I wouldn't let another man near my heart. He'd damaged it and used me, leaving me broken. He'd never loved me, and I had fallen for him, opening my heart to him and letting him in.

Greyson took my hand and brought it to his lips, kissing it softly. "Never."

He'd spoken the word with certainty and assuredness, and it worked its way into my soul, weaving through it and fortifying it. I searched his eyes, looking for any doubt but finding only clarity.

"I told you, Riley. You're mine. I won't hesitate to kill anyone who attempts to touch you."

Tipping my head, I wondered at his words. They were the same he'd said in his office. Kill was a strong word. One that gave me pause.

"Why do you have a key to my apartment, Greyson?"

He lifted me, lowering my feet to the floor before kissing me again. I couldn't help leaning into that kiss, my fingers running through his damp hair.

"Because I own this building, Riley. Because I wanted to spoil you and I wanted to play with you."

"You own this building?" I asked, ignoring the unease the last part of his statement brought me.

"Yes." He nipped at my lip and released me. I watched as he put his pants on, taking in the body I'd been unable to see in the dark. He was fit, the muscles defined in his chest and his legs. I knew he was older than me; I could tell by the gray around his temples and the hard lines that creased the corners of his eyes, the assured maturity with which he carried himself. But he looked fitter and sexier than most men my age.

He peeked up at me as he fixed his belt, raising his brow and giving me a cocky grin. The heat rose in my cheeks, and Greyson chuckled before his eyes perused my body the same way I'd just done to him. There was no bashfulness with the way his eyes devoured me, and my insides grew warm.

"Go clean up like a good girl before your coffee gets cold."

I stared at him, knowing my mouth had dropped. "You're not blaming cold coffee on me."

"I will if it gets cold." He crossed his arms, and I walked over to him, pressing my body into his, enjoying the warmth and solidness of him. I wrapped my hand around his neck and brought his mouth to mine, losing myself in his kiss once more before I walked away, feeling his eyes on my ass.

After a quick shower, I brazenly walked nude across my apartment hearing Greyson grumble about fucking me again if I didn't stop tempting him. I eyed him, considering the threat and thinking it wasn't one I cared to worry about. The way my belly flipped every time I thought about him inside of me, I could have let him fuck me all day.

Once I dressed, I sat at the table across from him, fingering the delicate bracelet he'd left me before I knew he was my stranger. "You know, breaking into an apartment and taking advantage of me could have gone very wrong."

"Maybe, but I didn't take advantage of you, Riley. If I recall, I got you off with my tongue that night after you gave me permission."

I clenched my legs, remembering the strange mix of fear, excitement, and satisfaction I'd experienced.

He looked down at his coffee, his expression softening as if he'd thought of something. "If I had to do it over again, I would have done it differently." He glanced up with that unguarded vulnerability before he looked away, setting his gaze out my window.

"It definitely left an impression," I muttered. "And...I can't say I didn't enjoy it."

He turned back to me, his eyes lighting. There were dimensions to Greyson Tides. Ones I didn't think he let show often, hiding himself under the serious exterior.

"What are we, Greyson? Am I just a game to you? Something for you to conquer before you move on to your next challenge?"

His expression hardened, and I realized I'd said the wrong thing. This was more to him, and my breath caught. He stood, resting his hands on either side of my chair and hovering over me. This was the side of Greyson Tides that left people saying his name in whispers, the powerful man who owned Bridgeville, the intense millionaire people feared and respected.

"What do you want us to be, Miss Brinks? Do you want me to leave? To make this a one-night stand and never come to your bed again? Never have you in my bed?"

My lungs burned with the breath that was still stuck in my chest. The thought of not having his touch again was like not having air to breathe.

"No," I mumbled, finding it hard to speak. His blue eyes were penetrating as he waited for me to say more. "I want to be yours." And I did. The fear of him walking out and not returning left me aching, and I knew then that I needed him. No matter how twisted this had started, I wanted to belong to him.

"Good girl," he said, causing my insides to clench. "Because I always get what I want, Riley. And I want you. I want you in my bed every night, my tongue against your clit, and your pussy around my cock."

"That's all?" I dared, knowing that wasn't enough for me. "Because that makes it sound like I'm just your whore."

He flinched like I'd slapped him, that reaction assuring me that his words had been his defense to cover what was below his tough façade.

"And I won't play the game if that's all you want," I continued.

His finger brushed along my cheek. "I want your smile. I want your laugh. I want the blush that climbs in your cheeks. I want the naïve woman who doesn't know how gorgeous she is or how she breaks me."

My breath fled from my lungs, my heart thudding so hard in my chest that he must have heard it. Reaching up, I pulled his lips to mine, kissing him. "I'm yours," I said against his lips as he drew me from the chair and into his arms. And I knew it was the truth. I belonged to Greyson Tides and would die before I let anything take me from him.

Chapter Seventeen

GREYSON

I didn't think there had ever been a time when I was as content as I was when Riley said she was mine. The words settled in my chest, weaving through my heart and clinging tight to it. Everything I'd initially wanted with her had fallen to the wayside like leaves blowing on a windy day. Even the way I'd imagined taking her was a lost thought because I wanted to be something different with her. She made me want to be different, to be the soft lover and leave the dominating prick I was every day aside.

I rose before dawn, running home to change and check on a few things. I'd promised her the day, which meant no work. And I never went a day without work. There was always something I needed to deal with. After showering, I called Den to find out the status of Clint Randall. There was still nothing. It gave me hope that the scumbag had gone back to his family with his tail between his legs, but that wasn't the way with the Bad Omens. They were relentless unless presented with an obstacle they couldn't surmount...like me.

After their run-in with me decades before, they kept to their province. I wouldn't have cared if they brought down Mason, but then I'd have them in my province, and I wanted them nowhere near anything of mine. So my threat had included the entire province, including Mason's territory—a threat they'd now challenged. I had every right to retaliate, but I needed my men here. Randall wouldn't quit because if he returned without his prize, his family would kill him. Mason was his job, and he would complete it. That meant he would come after anyone Mason loved.

"Hey," Riley said, drawing me back to the present.

I'd promised her I'd spend the day with her and had taken her to the seaside town of Cantwell, a quiet place with shops and history. Lights and garland decorated the streets and houses. This was the weekend of their Christmas market, which ran the length of the main street.

I took her hand in mine and pulled her to me, hating how much I loved the feel of her in my arms. Her green eyes were light as they searched mine.

"Where did you go?" she asked.

There was a comfort with her, as if she'd always been a part of my life. Always been mine.

"Just wondering what to get you for Christmas," I lied. "It's only two weeks away."

"More gifts, Greyson?"

Raising a brow, I said, "You don't like my gifts?"

She wrapped her arms around me. Her pink hat brought out the blush on her cheeks, giving her an innocent look. I brushed my knuckles over her cheek, feeling the warmth of it even in the cold. A snowflake dropped on her nose, and she smiled. My heart leaped in reaction, and I fought the need to pull from her, to push her away, because I knew what that meant. Knew I'd fallen too hard in the few weeks Riley had been in my life, even before I'd taken her the prior night. I wasn't sure how she had woven her way into my icy heart, but she had.

"I love your gifts," she replied softly. "But I already have everything I want."

"And what was it you wanted?"

"You."

That leap in my heart became a pounding I couldn't ignore, and I pulled her closer, kissing her and tasting her berry lip gloss. I'd been cold and heartless for too long, keeping everyone out, and Riley Brinks had obliterated that barrier, seeping into my heart and claiming it. The idea left me uncertain because this wasn't my life—walking the streets while holding hands and ignoring the threat that existed outside of my peaceful moment. My life was risky; it was violent and deadly. There were reasons I didn't let people in, and Mason Brinks was learning the hard way why loving someone was a liability.

"Grey?" Riley said, her voice layered with vulnerability.

"You know, no one calls me Grey," I scolded. She looked unsure, her demeanor changing, and I didn't like that I'd turned the moment like that. "But I like how you say it."

"So it's mine?"

"All yours. But I'm still getting you something better for Christmas. I'm not sure I count."

"You do," she whispered before pulling my lips to hers again.

We spent the day in Cantwell, and as night fell, I watched her reaction, loving how her eyes lit with excitement as the town became a winter wonderland. The snow had continued in light flurries, and they shimmered in the lights as they fell.

My phone rang, ruining the moment. We were in line for hot chocolate, so I excused myself, walking just far enough for privacy but close enough to keep her in sight. From my periphery, I spotted Tinge alongside another of my men, both on edge with my move. Riley hadn't questioned their presence, and I supposed having Mason as a brother normalized the constant need for security.

"Speak," I said to Alec.

"We found no trace of Randall in Bridgeville, but we found something."

My hand tightened on the phone. "Go on."

"He was in Creekwood."

My chest cinched, and I swept my eyes around Riley, suddenly on guard again.

"When?"

"That's the interesting part. Remember the day Riley was there?"

Fuck. My heart was hammering in my chest so hard I was worried Riley might hear it from where she stood.

"Well, he was there that day. There's footage of him inside the mall, but none outside."

"How close was he to her?"

"He was two tables away as she ate lunch."

"Dammit." I searched the crowd for any sign of him as Riley made her way back to me with her hands encasing her hot chocolate. "Double security in the city. I want eyes on every entrance in and every way out."

"Boss, Bad Omens are like ghosts. They remain hidden. You know what this means, right?"

"Yeah, he wanted to be seen. It was a message for Mason, one he missed." Riley was getting too close to talk any further. "Let me know if you find anything else."

I hung up just as she approached, giving me a smile over the rim of the cup while she blew on the liquid to cool it down.

"Everything okay?" she asked.

"Yeah, just a pest in an inconvenient place. I'll take care of it. We should probably head back."

Her brow lifted delicately. "Back...and what does that mean?"

Giving her a coy smile, I said, "It means you'll be sleeping in my bed tonight so I can use that body like I've been thinking of doing all day."

I wasn't about to let her return to her apartment, nor was I about to let her sleep alone.

"That sounds tempting, but..." There was a distinct seductive quality to her voice that reached in and tugged at my dick.

"But?"

"What if we don't go back yet?"

"Well then, that would delay my ability to touch you and rip that climax from you."

She shivered delectably. "Let's stay here. There's a bed-and-breakfast down the street—"

"Done," I said before she could finish. We were far enough from Bridgeville, and I could protect her if Randall was anywhere close. "Ready to turn in? Because I'm starving, and I know exactly what I want to eat."

Her blush returned, and I took her hand, leading her to the small bed-and-breakfast. It wasn't a place I usually would have stayed, but for Riley, I would. The reward of having her naked body against mine the entire night was worth the sacrifice.

I spent the night touching her, exploring every inch of her body as she explored mine and finding that even with as much as she blushed, Riley was far from shy. She was confident and aggressive when she wanted to be. By the time she fell asleep in my arms, she'd left me exhausted. I listened to her soft breaths as I held her and wondered at the effect she had on me. Wondered at the way she was claiming me and deciding that I was hers to claim.

RILEY WAS A LATE SLEEPER, which worked out perfectly because I was not. At dawn, I rose and made my way out to the porch, leaving one man stationed outside the room while Tinge followed me.

"What?" Mason answered in a cranky tone.

"Did I wake you, asshole?"

"Tides." His tone changed instantly.

"Your guy was in Creekwood."

I could sense the tension in the silence that followed. "When?" he finally asked.

"Recently. We pulled cameras and tracked his movements in the mall. Seems he sat at a table in the food court for a while but didn't eat. Not sure what he was looking at, but my guy said he was pretty intense." I knew what he was looking at, but I wasn't about to let Mason know I had Riley.

"Fuck. Any sign of him after that?"

"No. And we haven't seen him in the city. We'll keep searching. The prick won't make it past me if he dares step foot in Bridgeville." I didn't like the fact that he'd been in Creekwood. It fell under my territory, and that meant I had no choice now but to retaliate. My threat against the Bad Omens stood. They'd pay if they dared step foot in any part of my territory.

"What made you look at Creekwood?" he asked. Damn, he was smart, and I hoped that didn't send him looking for Riley here. He knew better than to cross into my city.

"I had my men start from the center of Bridgeville and work their way out into the smaller towns. I warned those derelicts that they weren't to take a step in any part of my territory, regardless of how far out it was from Bridgeville."

"Creekwood edges your territory and mine, Greyson. Don't get cocky and think it belongs to you."

I gritted my teeth. "It does," I said, not bothering to wait for his response and ending the call.

"All good, boss?" Tinge asked.

"It will be in a few minutes," I said, eliciting a laugh from him.

Rolling the tension from my shoulders, I returned to the room. Riley was still sleeping soundly, but I was restless. My instinct was gnawing at me that I was missing something, that Clint Randall was out there threatening to hurt my girl.

Kicking my shoes off, I crawled back into the bed, kissing her shoulder and neck. She stirred, turning over, her eyes lazily blinking open. A dazzling smile filled her face as she raised her hand and cupped my cheek. I leaned into it, enraptured by how that touch lit my heart.

"Good morning," she murmured.

"It's about to be," I replied, kissing her.

"You're dressed," she complained, her hands running down my shirt.

"Is that a problem?"

She tugged at my shirt. "It is because I need you naked."

Chuckling, I sat back, removing my shirt and perusing her naked body. She eyed my pants, and I couldn't help laughing again.

"You are a demanding thing, aren't you?"

"I have certain expectations," she replied as I rose and slowly removed my pants.

She sat up, scooting to the side of the bed, and watched me.

"Better?" I asked, moving closer to her.

Her hand ran the length of my chest, causing sparks to blaze through me. "Better."

I wanted her again. I didn't think there would ever be a time when I wouldn't crave Riley, especially now that I'd had her. Putting aside the concerns, the worries, and the threat that lingered in the distance, I leaned down and picked her up, pulling her against me and kissing her. Her legs wrapped around me, and my body responded, coming alive with her touch. Sitting on the edge of the bed, I guided her body so that she enveloped me. She was drenched, and my dick twitched at the feel of her around it. I brought my hands down her body to hold her waist as she rose and fell over me. Our kisses never stopped even as my need for release rose, taking over until it was a tsunami threatening to drown me.

Threading my hands through her hair, I wondered at how she brought the gentle side of me out. I'd imagined pulling her hair and forcing her moves, but those thoughts fled as soon as I touched her, maybe even before. Because all I wanted to do to Riley was make love to her. To hear her cries, to feel her come undone in my arms, to bring her pleasure.

As my climax tore through me, she came, her cry intertwining with mine, and I knew then that I never wanted to hear anyone's cry but hers, never wanted to feel anyone come undone for me but her. I held her against me while the ripples of my release drifted through me. Her body trembled when my hand skimmed up her back to weave through her hair.

When our lips finally parted, she leaned back to study me. The look in her eyes penetrated what remained of my hard shell and crumbled it, my heart becoming hers completely in that moment.

I brushed her hair back, slipping my fingers through the ebony strands. Her green eyes were rich as they searched mine, and I broke, knowing she had claimed me, just as she had on that first day I'd seen her.

"I love you, Riley," I said, speaking the words I hadn't said in years. Words that had never had real meaning until now. Words that had always felt empty, but with Riley, they had definition.

Her eyes sparkled, her smile growing.

"Is it possible to love a person you don't really know?" she asked, and I frowned, not sure how to answer the question because I knew every part of her. But she didn't know that. It was a secret I'd have to share at some point and hope it didn't ruin what we had. And she didn't know me because no one knew me. I never let anyone in. "Because, if so, I love you, too, Mr. Tides."

My smile was one I couldn't have stopped if I'd wanted. It lit every part of my body, and I pulled her to me, kissing her deeply.

I'd expected to use Riley, to fuck her, to taste her, then break her. But I'd never expected to love her, to crave her like I'd wanted no one before, to have her break me. And that's precisely what she'd done.

RILEY WAS STANDING in my bedroom window, looking out at the snow on the ground below. The rumpled sheets on my bed showed the only sign that I'd made love to her the prior night, falling asleep to the soothing sound of her breaths as she slept on my chest. I'd risen early, knowing her sleeping patterns now. It had been three days since the Christmas party, three days and nights of knowing she was wholly mine.

After leaving her to sleep, I hit the gym on the lower level of my house, my hour on the bike fueled by thoughts of Riley. It had been too early to wake her, so I spent the next hour checking in with Alec, then taking care of a few loose ends. When I returned to my room, I took a moment to observe her. She had put on my white button-down shirt, the bottom touching the top of her knees, the sleeves too long to do more than hang loose. She looked sexy and adorable at once.

I liked her there, in my home, in my clothes, in my bed. It was where she belonged and where she would be safest, but I couldn't tell her that yet. It was too soon. Although with the threat of Clint Randall out there, I'd be broaching the subject soon, no matter how much she complained.

I slid my hands around her waist, loving how she leaned back into my chest.

"Where were you?" she asked, her hand raising to touch my cheek. I turned my head into it and kissed her palm.

"I had a quick workout, then made a few calls."

She peeked over at me, her green eyes twinkling in the

morning light. "So you're all sweaty?" she asked, wrinkling her nose.

"No more than you had me last night," I replied.

Nibbling at her neck, I pushed the sleeve of the shirt down, kissing her shoulder and sliding my hand down to caress her breast.

"Have I been a good girl?"

I pushed the shirt further down, pulling her hair to the side and kissing the back of her neck. She shivered, my pulse racing in response.

"Oh, baby girl, you've been a very good girl."

Her sigh reached deep inside of me, my cock bucking at the sound of it. My fingers skirted down her back, tracing her scar. I heard the slight hitch of her breath. She didn't need to tell me who had given her that scar. I knew a knife wound when I saw one. I'd noticed it and the others—one behind her neck and another low enough to have punctured a lung—when I'd first explored her body, but I hadn't asked about them. She'd yet to divulge anything about her past or her brother and I'd yet to push because I had my own secrets.

Lingering on the one on her back, I asked, "What are your scars from?" curious to hear her answer.

She went rigid, and I moved my fingers around her, cupping her breast and feeling her relax, her nipple rising to my touch.

"An accident about a year ago," she mumbled.

"Huh, an accident where you ran into a knife blade?" I pushed.

"Something like that," she answered, turning to me.

She eyed my gray t-shirt and sweats. "I like this look," she said, pushing my shirt up and running her hands up my chest.

"It's hard to work out in a dress shirt," I muttered, her touch leaving me longing for more.

She pushed further, and I took the hint, looking forward to more of that touch, even if she was using it to divert my attention.

I tugged the shirt over my head, her fingers tracing my abs and causing my stomach to knot in anticipation. Weaving my fingers through her hair, I brought my lips to hers, expecting this to escalate. Her fingertips settled over my own scar, and she mumbled, "And where did you get this scar?"

Her green eyes challenged me. She knew that as much as she kept secrets from me, I guarded my own. And I was learning quickly that my girl was a vixen, even if she looked sweet and innocent on the surface.

I drew back, irritated that she'd stopped my pleasure and debating if I should punish her for it. I wasn't in the mood, and I hadn't tested how amenable she'd be to letting me completely dominate her. She broke me so easily that I'd been nothing but soft with her, losing all resolve to be anything more because of it.

"An accident about twenty years ago," I answered, mimicking her answer to me.

She traced the bullet wound that had changed my life. No bullet had touched me since. I'd hired the best sharp shooters money could buy, training until my shot was quick and lethal every time. Ensuring my enemies knew never to fuck with me again. I'd never taken a chance after that, doubling my security and becoming the most calculated, feared boss in all the territories. And no one had dared go against me again.

I stopped her hand, her emerald eyes glancing back up at me.

"We both have our secrets, don't we, baby girl?"

Her mouth parted, and I brushed my thumb over her bottom lip.

"Yes," she breathed, her tongue sweeping around my thumb. She was diverting my attention again, and I intended to let her because that move had me so hard, my pants were tenting. I'd yet to experience her mouth around me, but I was a patient man, and I knew when she finally dropped to her knees like I'd imagined before my game had morphed to forever, that she'd be worth the wait.

She dropped my shirt from her shoulders, her eyes mischievous, and my dick jumped like it did anytime I even thought of that body.

"Are you trying to distract me, Riley?"

"I'm not trying," she replied, her lip curving deliciously.

I wrapped my hand around her neck, pulling her against me with more force than usual, and her eyes lit. I knew the day would come when I'd test that reaction, see if she welcomed my aggression like I thought she would, but for now I let it simmer, releasing her neck and finding her lips. Her kiss set my soul on fire, my desire for her flaring.

I skimmed her curves and grabbed her ass, lifting her. She didn't hesitate to wrap her legs around me as I walked her to the wall, her kisses becoming increasingly more feral with each step. Shoving her back to the wall, I tugged my cock free and rested it in her folds, the warmth almost too inviting to ignore.

She whined, shimmying her body to envelop me, but I stopped her, sliding through her as she grew more soaked. Frustrated, she pushed against my chest, complaining. With a tsk, I pinned her hands above her head.

"Don't make me tie you up again," I warned, her eyes shimmering with excitement.

"But I want you inside of me."

I grinned, loving how desperate she sounded. "And I want you so close to coming that you're clenching around me when I'm fucking you. Now settle down before I spank you."

The inhale she took was beautiful, her arousal soaking me more. I was looking forward to discovering all the ways my girl liked to play. I returned to sliding through her wetness, dropping my mouth to her breast and sucking on her nipple. Riley's breasts were small but firm and perfect for sucking. They'd quickly become one of my favorite parts of her body, and I loved how she responded when I touched them. Soon she was trembling so hard I could tell she was close.

Keeping her arms pinned above her head, I drove into her just as she fell apart, her body clamping so tight around me it almost took me over the edge with her. I thrust through it, relishing her cries as my mouth fought to smother them. Her legs were tight around my waist, her heels pressing me deeper. I had her arms still locked above her head, my body slamming her into the wall with each thrust. My desire for release was climbing and I could feel another climax building in her.

"That's it, be a good girl and come for me again," I demanded, my mouth against her ear.

My words pushed her over the edge, her body convulsing, her muscles bearing down around me so that I lost control, filling her as my orgasm surged through me with a force that left my knees shaking.

When I could finally function again, I released her wrists from my grasp, and slid from her warmth. She drew my head down, kissing me sensually and stirring my craving for her again.

"You better stop that, or we won't leave this room all day," I warned.

Her lips pouted, and I nibbled on the bottom one before I stepped from her.

"I need to work, and you need to be here naked and waiting for me when I return."

Her expression shifted, her eyes narrowing, and a distinctive hiss escaped through her teeth.

"You don't like that idea?" I asked, fixing my pants and picking my shirt up.

"I need to work, too. And I'm not some trophy piece you can keep in your bed to fuck at your convenience."

She snatched the button-down she'd been wearing from the floor, oblivious to the ire that was building in me.

"You no longer have a job," I said, my teeth grinding. She whipped her head toward me. "You can't fuck the owner of the company all weekend and expect to show up at the office the next

Monday." My words were harsh, but her insinuation that I wanted her for convenience had soured my mood.

Her face fell. "That's right," she mumbled. "But I need to work, Greyson. I can't just sit around all day."

"Waiting to fuck me at my convenience?" I groused.

Her eyes snapped up, realization setting in them. "I'm sorry. I didn't mean it that way."

"No? And how did you mean it? Is that what you think, even after Cantwell?"

I hated how vulnerable I sounded, how her words had wounded me. She walked over to me, her fingers caressing my cheek.

"No, it's not," she said, a deep sigh slipping from her. "I know that's not what you want. That you love me, even if you fell in love with me in a creepy way," she added, her tone playful.

I scowled, not ready to reciprocate.

"I love you, Grey. But I can't sit around playing house while you work. It's not in my nature. I need to keep busy. I need to work and I promise I'll still be in your bed or my bed, naked and ready for you to take me."

I yanked her to me, taking the shirt from her hand.

"I'll find you something, but you can't work in my firm."

"And you'll let me go back to my apartment?"

My jaw clenched. I didn't want her out of my sight, but I still had the cameras set up so I could monitor her, and I could have her guarded when I couldn't be with her.

"Yes, but with security."

"Security? Is that necessary? It's bad enough they follow us everywhere. Why do they do that, anyway?" Her brow had furrowed, suspicion sitting within her eyes.

"I'm worth a lot of money, Riley. I need security and now that you're part of my life, you do, too."

I wasn't certain she bought the excuse, but she didn't question it.

"Fine," she muttered, trying to move from my hold.

"Where do you think you're going?" I asked.

"You need to get ready for work and I need to find a job."

"I'll find you a job." I noticed how the crease between her brows deepened. "But I need a shower first."

She struggled to free herself from my arms, but I held her tight.

"Go shower then," she complained. "And let me go."

"I want you in that shower, Riley. That water needs to be warm and soaking your naked body before I walk in."

She shivered, relaxing into my hold.

"Then you'll turn that ass around, like a good girl, so I can punish you for that earlier comment."

Her brow raised as her lips pursed.

"I think a few good slaps to that ass should suffice before I fuck you again."

Her eyes had grown so large, the emerald was breathtaking. I released her and turned her toward the bathroom, giving her a loud smack on her ass. Her squeal was like her hand on my cock, and it leaped to life again. "Start moving, baby girl, before I add to my count."

She peered over her shoulder at me, her hand rubbing her ass cheek. The look she gave me had my stomach flipping, and I returned it with a devious grin to match the hunger in those eyes.

I made good on my promise, delivering enough light slaps to leave her completely soaked and me so hard it ached before I yanked her hips back and took her there, the water pouring over us and muting our satisfied groans.

Chapter Eighteen

RILEY

Greyson sat across from me at my small table. My mouth was unflatteringly agape as I stared at him.

"Are you serious? It's too early for that, isn't it? I mean, it's only been a little over a week."

His smirk made my legs turn to jelly. "Well, if you count the times I had you tied up, it's been longer than that."

I pursed my lips, shooting him my most annoyed look, which only caused him to chuckle.

"Greyson, I can't move in with you this fast."

He'd suggested it over our morning coffee. He'd already insisted I quit my job for conflict reasons. It didn't look good to be fucking one of his employees and breaking his own dating rule. Instead, he set me up at the small boutique firm I'd initially interviewed with. There was something about how he made all the arrangements for me, like Mason had done, that I wasn't comfortable with. I hadn't known Mason had gotten me the position in Treemont until our fight, but the truth had burned. I had my degree in finance, and I was good at what I did. I'd even interned at one of the larger firms in the city. But he'd set it all up, like he'd done everything in my life. The internship had probably been him pulling strings as well.

Now Greyson was doing the same thing, treating me like I couldn't function on my own.

"It makes sense, Riley." He sat back and crossed his arms, ignoring the daggers in my eyes.

"No," I said, sitting back and mimicking him.

He raised his brow, his jaw ticking. "No?"

"No."

Leaning forward, he rested his elbows on the table, his hands clenching. "No one says no to me, Riley. It comes with repercussions when they do."

If those repercussions involved a spanking, I would be happy to rebel. Every time his hand met my ass, it left me soaked.

Giving him a defiant glare, I said, "Well, I just did."

I'd never seen his muscles so strained. I was resisting him, and he didn't like it. And he didn't know what to do about it. I was enjoying the power play and wished I'd said no to Mason more often. It had taken me years of being told what to do to find that confidence.

"You're an aggravating woman," he grumbled.

"I know, but you're not changing my mind."

He stood, the chair sliding back as he ran his hand through his hair and muttered, "Fuck."

That's when I saw there was more to his request. Worry sat on his shoulders. I could see it in the tension that rolled from his neck and onto his back.

"Then you stay at my place more often," he finally said.

I'd only been there twice. It was cold and held no personality.

"I like it here. My bed is big enough for both of us."

He glared at me. "That's my compromise, Riley."

Laughing, I said, "That's a compromise? Move in with me or spend every night at my place?"

"I didn't say every night. I said more."

I pursed my lips. "Your place is cold and sterile."

"Then decorate it," he said. "Cover it in fairy lights and puffy blankets like your apartment. I don't care. I want you there, Riley."

Standing, I walked to him, taking his hand in mine and feeling the tension there. "Is there something you're not telling me, Grey?"

His jaw tightened, and I could see the conflict in his eyes.

"You know," I said. "If I'm going to decorate your house in fairy lights and fluffy pink blankets, I need you to open up more."

He looked down at my hand in his and fingered the bracelet I never took off. The one with the delicate peonies that sat softly on my skin.

"You'll move in?" he asked.

"No. I won't have you lead my life, Greyson. I...it reminds me too much of my brother."

"You have a brother?" he asked quickly.

"I told you we didn't know enough about each other," I said, flashing him a smile.

He sat and pulled me to his lap. "Tell me about your brother."

"There's not much to tell. We're...we're estranged. I don't talk to him anymore."

I looked away, but he eased my face back to him. "Why not?"

"Because of the shit you're pulling and, well, he's not the man I thought he was. He lied to me about a lot of things, and I found out the hard way. Getting hurt in the process."

"So that's why you left Treemont?" he asked, rubbing his hand down my thigh.

"Yes. There was a situation that turned bad, and none of it would have happened if he had been honest with me." I looked away again, not wanting to relive the pain. The fear the memory of those two days held. The way Clint had turned on me, using me only to get to Mason. I still didn't know what had hurt more:

the pain from knowing he'd used me, the pain of his fists and the knife wounds, or the pain of learning Mason's secrets.

"Riley," Greyson said softly.

"I'm fine. I don't want to talk about it. Do you have siblings?" I said, turning the questions to him.

He let out a long sigh before saying, "I have a brother. Correction, I had a brother."

I creased my brow. "He's dead?" I asked, my heart breaking for him.

"No," he said, with the shake of his head. "But he's dead to me and I'm dead to him. We had a falling out twenty years ago."

I waited for more, wondering if it could be any worse than my falling out with Mason.

"Over a woman."

I gritted my teeth, the thought stirring an envy I didn't like.

"That's cute. I might ease up on my punishment if you keep that jealousy thing up," he teased.

"Punishment?"

The memory of his smacks to my ass returned, warmth rushing between my legs. He'd followed every one with the firm smoothing of his hand over the sting, his body pressing mine into the tile wall as he breathed in ragged exhales close to my ear. I'd come so hard when he finally mumbled a 'good girl' and jerked my hips back and penetrated me, I could barely remain upright.

He didn't answer me. Instead, a wicked gleam filled his eyes. His hand moved up my back before it slid down my arm and encompassed my wrist.

"Oh," I breathed, a fire heating in my belly. He was distracting me, and it was working. "What woman?" I asked, needing to fight for my control back.

"A beautiful redhead I stole from him. He didn't like it when he found her mouth around my cock, and we haven't talked since. I saved him. She was a bitch who needed to be put in her place."

I cringed at the visual he'd put in my mind, not liking the

thought of another woman touching him. But the harsh way he'd spoken surprised me. It was crass and heartless. He must have noticed my reaction, his eyes crinkling with humor.

"You don't like my language?"

"No, I don't."

He laughed harder. "Says the woman who told me to fuck her when I had her tied up."

Butterflies skittered through my stomach. He tightened his grip on my wrist, bringing my other one behind me, and my breath hitched. "What do you say I give you that punishment now?"

I couldn't help the way my body pressed toward him at his words. Aside from the few smacks to my ass, he'd been nothing but gentle with me, although there was a force behind his gentle moves, a strength that was Greyson.

His phone rang, and his expression hardened. With a sigh, he let go of my wrists and lifted me from him. I gave him a frown, my disappointment clear, but he only kissed my nose and walked out of the apartment.

"Speak," I heard him say as the door shut.

He established the rule that first day—the phone would not go to voicemail, and he would take all calls away from me. He didn't mix business with pleasure he'd told me, but I didn't buy that.

I chewed my bottom lip, thinking about his proposition of moving in with him. While it seemed soon, and I wanted to maintain my independence, the idea made me tingle inside. This powerful man, who could have any woman in the city, wanted me. And he wanted me enough to have me live with him.

It was dreamy, and if Mason hadn't burned me, I would have considered it. I cracked the door, hearing Greyson come down the hall. He was yelling at someone, and the sound sent a chill down my spine.

"I don't give a fuck, look again. I want him found and if he steps foot in Bridgeville, I want to know."

I backed away from the door as he pushed it open. His blue eyes were dark and hard, and I took a step back. I'd seen that look before and it was one that brought back nightmares I'd submerged beneath the façade of strength I'd built.

His expression changed, softening to the man I loved, his blue eyes brightening as they widened with realization. He stopped and studied me before looking down at his phone. "I need to be tough, Riley. Respect is earned, and it's hard to keep. There's a reason I'm as powerful as I am, a reason I own this city."

He lifted his eyes back to me.

"And what reason is that?" I asked.

"Because people fear me." He walked closer to me, running his hand through my hair. "But you don't need to fear me. I'll never hurt you."

I searched his eyes, looking for any sign of doubt, any sense that he was lying to me because I'd heard those words before. From my brother, from Clint. And they'd lied.

He put the phone on the table and took his shoes off. I cocked my brow, giving him a questioning look. "Don't you need to go to the office?"

"I don't have a schedule and I believe punishment is due for telling me no."

I inhaled sharply, the air burning my lungs as he rolled his sleeves up. Warmth seeped between my legs when he walked to me and pulled my shirt over my head. My stomach quivered in anticipation, but he stepped back.

"Take the pants off, Riley."

I held his gaze and pushed my jeans off.

"On the bed, like a good girl." My legs clenched. He'd never been commanding before, but that good girl drenched me every time he said it. This side of him reminded me of the nights he'd sneaked into my apartment.

I walked over and crawled onto my bed, but as I tried to turn over, he yanked me back to my knees. Every nerve in my body quivered in expectation. Slowly, he removed my thong, sliding his hand up my leg and dipping his fingers between my legs. I moaned, throwing my head back, but he moved behind me and pushed my head down. There was no force, just the gentle strength that was Greyson. Moves that never brought me pain or fear, only pleasure. He pushed the strap of my bra down and cupped my breast as his fingers slid to my clit, rubbing my wetness over it.

"Do you want to come, baby girl?" he murmured, pressing his length against me. His clothes were still on, but I could feel how hard he was.

I wanted him to take me again, to bring me the release his fingers were building in me. I groaned into my sheets as it climbed, my body quivering until I was so close I knew I would fall. But he removed his fingers, leaving me aching.

"You haven't been a good girl, Riley."

"Greyson," I whined.

I tried picking my head up, but he forced my shoulders back down, pressing further into me. He pulled my bra strap further more cupping my breast and brushing his thumb across my nipple.

"You need to understand that I don't like the word no, baby girl."

My moan was muffled but loud, my entire body quivering as he bit my shoulder, saying, "Beg me, Riley."

The command fueled the unfulfilled release that was pulsing to be freed. He dragged his teeth over my shoulder, his hand skimming the length of my body before he plunged his fingers back into me. My entire body lurched, the need to climax crashing for a way out, so close my legs could barely hold me up.

"Tell me what you want," he demanded, his teeth scraping my ass, his fingers falling from me and leaving me so empty it hurt.

"Make me come, Greyson," I begged. "Please."

His hands left my body, my cry loud and anguished until they spread over my back, his fingers threading in my hair and pausing there before sliding over my neck. I moaned again, wondering if he would leave it there.

He leaned back over me. "I think you're forgiven," he said. I shuddered, knowing he was finally going to bring me the release I was craving. His fingers twitched, almost tightening around my neck before they drifted over my body, softly caressing my breast then moving over my stomach, slowly, tantalizing me with the expectation. And when he brushed my clit, his other hand coming around my hip, two fingers penetrating me, I lost it. My climax shredded me with its force, my hoarse cry echoing through the room.

I didn't have time to even take control of my body when I heard his zipper, followed by the fullness of him as he drove into me. His growl was loud, almost feral, and had me trembling. My body was a storm brewing and waiting to explode as he pounded into me. He'd never taken me this hard, and the force of it sent my climax tumbling. I shattered again, coming so hard he had to hold my hips up while he continued to drive into me with abandon.

"That's a good girl," he said. "Fuck, that feels good."

I picked myself up and threw my hair back, feeling his hand reach up to thread through it. I could tell he was holding back. He wanted to pull it but didn't want to be aggressive with me. But damn, I wanted him to be rough this time. I needed to feel all he could bring. To know the side of him he hid from me.

"Pull it," I purred, and he growled, his fingers wrapping tight and pulling until I was arching forward.

A rush of stimulating tingles hit me, my body alight with the sensation. I let out a cry, loving the side of him that fed the bad girl in me, the one who needed him to own me in only the way he could. He tightened his hold on my hip, thrusting into me so hard I could barely catch my breath. The thrill of it sent my climax climbing again, a fire burning me from the inside. An uncontrollable blaze that Greyson was about to unleash. The way he was clinging to my hip while his other hand remained entangled in my hair, accompanied by the grunts he was emitting, tore my release from me. I lost control, coming with an intensity that had me screaming. He let out a growl, breaking with me and pulling my hair so hard that my body lifted, my back hitting his chest. My orgasm was pummeling me, and he wrapped his arm around me, pushing deep into me until he stilled. The tremors that were rippling through me made it hard to breathe, and I clung to his thighs, trying to gain some control. Loosening his grip, he let me go and I dropped to the bed, peeking over at him as he fell next to me.

His breaths were ragged and sexy, the completely satisfied look on his face worth the throbbing in my scalp. He rested his hand on his chest and glanced at me, his eyes questioning me.

"You assumed I don't like it hard," I said, giving him a shrug.

"Shit. You've been holding out on me."

I leaned over his chest and kissed him. "I don't want that all the time. Just when you're fired up and yelling at your employees."

He chuckled and pulled my lips to his, kissing me ravenously until the kiss softened and the lover I knew returned.

"Sure you don't want to wake up in my bed every morning? I can promise you my punishments will have you coming repeatedly now that I know you've been holding out on me," he said against my lips.

"I'm sure, but you already have me coming repeatedly." And more than any man had ever made me come.

"I'm only just starting," he said, rolling me from him and rising.

I watched as he tucked himself away and realized he had taken none of his clothes off, and I was lying there just in my bra. The thought added a heightened level of naughtiness to how he'd taken me.

He put his shoes and coat on, then picked up his phone, giving me a devious grin before heading out to work. I dropped my head back. I didn't know what to think of Greyson. He wouldn't let me in, but he was slowly showing me who he was. There was no question I was in love with him. Just the thought of him sent quivers through my body.

Glancing at the clock, I knew I had to get moving. Greyson had scheduled a meeting for me with the local firm I'd originally planned to interview before his firm tempted me. I cleaned myself and dressed, opting for a flattering pair of black slacks and a stylish wrap shirt I'd picked up with the money Greyson had given me for my furniture. I shook my head at how sneaky he'd been as I locked my door, glancing over at Ava's apartment and wishing I could share my news with her. She'd left right before the Christmas party to spend the holidays with her family. I'd have plenty to tell her when she returned and could only imagine the sheer look of shock she'd have at the news that Greyson Tides now belonged to me just as much as I belonged to him.

I pulled my collar up against the cold as I exited the building. It had snowed the night before, but the sidewalks were clear, and my boots had chunky heels, so I didn't worry about slipping. I knew Greyson had his security on me, but I didn't see them. Wherever they were, they were discreet enough to go unnoticed by even me. The constant need for bodyguards reminded me of Mason's men, always close by, always on watch. He'd given the same excuse when I'd asked him about them many years ago. We had money, and that meant we needed protection. It had seemed like a simple answer back then, before I discovered the true reason he needed protection.

I let the thought go, shaking the idea that Greyson was anything like my brother. He was a businessman. My brother was a criminal who had done nothing but lie to me. I turned my thoughts back to Greyson and the way he'd let loose today, showing me the side he'd kept reserved. My stomach somersaulted, remembering how his fingers had felt tangled in my hair and forcing my head back.

As I approached my destination, I remained in a daze, the glow of my orgasms still lifting my mood and the residual of Greyson's touch leaving me warm. But a strange feeling of dread slipped in as I drew nearer to the office. A familiar fear sat in the back of my mind, causing the hairs to rise on my neck. I glanced around, not seeing anything but random people walking behind me. Turning back, I perused the oncoming walkers, but nothing caught my eye. I hurried my pace, a sense of urgency behind my steps. My heart was beating hard in my chest, and as I opened the door to the building, there was a movement in my periphery. I glanced up. Clint's cold brown eyes stared at me from down the street. He didn't move. He just stood there, leaning on the side of the building, staring at me. He tipped his head toward me, giving me an evil grin before Tom, the manager of the firm, pulled my attention away.

"Miss Brinks?" Tom said. "Is everything okay?"

Only then did I realize I'd dropped my bag, my hand gripping so tight to the door that my gloves had ripped. I looked back to find Clint gone, but the fear that had strangled me remained. Tom bent down and picked up my bag, handing it to me, his kind eyes evaluating me.

I willed myself to nod and made up an excuse of feeling dizzy. All the while, my mind was screaming in fear. Clint had found me, and he was here to finish the job. I'd fled Mason, leaving my protection behind and handing myself over to Clint like a lamb at slaughter.

I stared at my screen, seeing the blur of words but not paying attention to them. Riley was on my mind, as usual. She amazed me more every day. The way she'd asked me to pull her hair, reacting so beautifully to how hard I took her, had my cock aching. Other than the day I'd dominated her in the shower, I'd been nothing but gentle with her because she brought that out in me, but knowing she might be willing to satisfy some of those dirty thoughts I'd had about her early on was tantalizing.

Deciding that the numbers weren't being reviewed today, I rose and walked to my window, looking out at the wooded landscape behind my house. The snow left it a winter wonderland that would be the perfect backdrop for Christmas morning. Riley didn't know it yet, but she'd be staying with me on Christmas Eve. She may have stubbornly rejected my idea of moving in with me, but there was no way I was leaving her alone that night knowing it was her first Christmas away from her brother. I'd keep her mind off him. I had already made reservations for an elegant dinner, and her gifts were wrapped and ready.

It occurred to me that I didn't have a tree. I never paid much attention to holidays, but if I wanted to surprise her, I needed a tree. I reached for my phone, ready to call Sherry and have her find me one, when Riley's number appeared on the screen. It was only a few minutes after ten and she was supposed to be interviewing with Thomas Ren, the manager of the boutique firm she'd initially interviewed with. It was a formality. He would hire her because I'd told him to. But she wanted to maintain her independence, so the formalities needed to be kept in place.

"Riley?" I answered, curious as to why she would call so soon.

"Can you come pick me up?" Her voice was shaking and carried a familiar tone to it—fear.

My alarms went up. "What happened?"

"I'm just not feeling well, that's all. I don't think I can walk back and...I don't want to be alone." Those words told me everything because Riley was too independent to ever admit that. Something had spooked her.

"Where are you?"

"I'm at the firm."

"I'll be there. Stay in the office."

I hung up, rushing from my home and speeding into town. Every minute that passed was agonizing, and I tapped my steering wheel at each light. Pulling into a no-parking zone, I hopped from my car and rushed into the building.

"Thomas," I greeted him, seeing the concern etched in the worry lines on his forehead.

"She's in my office. She had a dizzy spell when she was walking in."

I hurried past him and into his office. Riley had her head in her hands, and I kneeled before her, taking her hands in mine. They were shaking, and as she raised her face, I didn't need to ask what had happened. I could see it in the fear that lined her eyes. I gritted my teeth, trying to maintain my calm for her.

"Can we go back to your place?" she asked.

"Of course." I brought her up and wrapped her in my arms, guiding her out of the building and into my car.

"What happened, Riley?" I asked as I drove.

She was staring out the window, her hands wrung, and I could see the tension in her posture. I needed to know if my suspicion that Clint Randall was here was correct, but I couldn't ask her because it was a part of her life she hadn't told me about. She continued to push for us to know more about our pasts, but she was as unwilling to give details as I was. We were both hiding the parts of ourselves that connected us to each other.

"I..." Waiting for her to continue, I held my breath, not wanting to hear that Randall had gotten through my defenses. "I thought I saw something."

"Something? Like what, Riley?" I was trying to keep my voice calm.

"It was nothing," she said, and I cursed her obstinance. Why wouldn't she let me into that part of her life?

Because she didn't know I could protect her. She didn't know who I was or what I was capable of—the body count that littered my past, the reason people side-stepped me, the reason they feared saying my name.

I glanced behind me, seeing Tinge trailing me with Den in the passenger seat. My men were always around me. I kept them more discreet than Riley's brother did, but they were there. I wondered why they hadn't spotted Randall. I'd deliberately left Den to guard her. If Riley had seen him, then Den would have. But he would have called me the minute he'd seen something, which told me Randall had only let Riley see a glimpse of him, enough to fuck with her but not enough for us to notice him.

The thing that made Bad Omens such piranha was their ability to hide in the shadows, to remain coiled and ready to strike when least expected. They were ghosts with killer instincts.

I gripped the steering wheel as I pulled up to the house. The home I kept just outside the city was a tall brownstone set in a row of others. I owned each one, and when my men weren't on duty, they were in them, ready to move at the first sign of trouble.

Opening the door, I ushered Riley inside. My men would reinforce the perimeter of the house without Riley noticing. I brought her to my couch and sat her down, stooping before her. She was so pale that she looked fragile, and it hurt to see her like that. Riley had a strength to her that I loved. The sparkle in her eyes was missing, and I vowed I would slaughter Randall myself and watch the life flee from his body.

I tipped her chin, and she gave me a small smile.

"Why don't you rest, baby girl? I'll start a fire and you can close your eyes. When you're ready to tell me what happened, I'll be here."

She nodded, and I rose, kissing her head before I got her a blanket. She curled into the couch as I started a fire and was sleeping by the time I finished. Leaving her to sleep, I strode to my office and closed the door, calling Den.

"What happened?"

"I don't know. Everything was fine when I was trailing her, but she started looking around the closer she got to the building. I had to step back so she wouldn't see me, and when I got the chance to move again, she'd dropped her bag, and Tom was helping her into the building. I searched the crowd and scoured the block when she was inside, but I didn't see anything."

"Fuck. He's here. I know that's what she saw. She just won't tell me. Somehow, he got past our defenses."

He was quiet for a minute before he said, "Unless he's been here the entire time."

The claw of fear that strangled my heart was enough to steal my breath. If that were the case, he knew everything she'd been doing. Every detail of her life, including me. But that in itself should have been enough to make him back off.

I ran a hand down my face. "Make sure everyone is on high alert. If that's the case, he's had time to watch me and find any weakness in my defenses. Make sure there are none."

"Yes, boss."

I disconnected, debating on whether I cared if Mason knew right before I hit his number.

"What," he answered.

"Always so cordial, Mason."

"Tides, I hope you're only bothering me because you have news."

"We spotted your man. He's in my city, and he seems to be hunting for something. Is there something you're not telling me, Brinks?"

He was quiet, and his silence spoke for him.

"What's he hunting?" I wanted to needle him. "What else is in my city?"

"Who," he said, and I could hear how clenched his jaw was. "He's hunting someone. Fuck. You need to let me in Bridgeville. I don't give a shit about territory."

I had him riled up, and I was enjoying the leverage over him, the fear pummeling him because he now realized where Riley was and that his monster was in the same place. What he didn't know was that I would viciously kill anyone who dared lay a hand on her. I wasn't hunting the piece of shit for Mason; I was hunting him for Riley.

"I'm not letting you in my city and don't even think about setting foot here. Who's he looking for?"

"It's not your business. Let me in the fucking city, Tides."

"Your desperation makes you sound pathetic, Brinks."

"I don't give a fuck what I sound like!" He was livid, and I was enjoying every minute.

"I'm not letting you in. Now tell me who he's here for."

He went silent for a moment before muttering, "No one. Just make sure he dies before he does any damage."

He hung up before I could say anything more. I'd found Mason's weakness. It was one I'd surmised he had when Riley moved here. At that time, I would have loved the position in which I currently had him pinned and I would have sent him both Randall's dead body and Riley's broken heart, her body soiled. But she'd changed all that, and now I would die before I hurt her.

I dropped back in my seat, running my hands through my hair. Randall was an issue, a bullet flying through the streets of my city and aimed at the woman I loved. And he'd done to her what I'd intended to do, breaking her heart, leaving her wounded, and with his fucking cum inside of her. I punched my desk, imagining the painful way I'd kill the son of a bitch for touching her.

Leaving my office, I checked on Riley, brushing her hair from her face and pulling the blanket further over her. I didn't like how fragile she looked; it hurt too much. For the first time in my life, fear had its claws in me, and I couldn't shake free of them. Randall had been so close to her. Close enough to hurt her before Den could have protected her. What if he did it again? As good as my men were, as tough as I was, there was still a slim probability. One I didn't like. Randall had hurt Riley under Mason's watch, and as much as I liked to taunt Mason, he was like me in many ways. If Randall got through his defenses, he could break through mine. I'd die before I let him hurt her, but that risk was one I wouldn't take.

Picking up the phone, I resolved myself to letting my control slide for Riley's sake.

"Where are you?" I asked Mason before he could say anything.

"Creekwood."

He was only a few hours away, searching for Riley and Randall, oblivious that they were so close until I'd called him.

"So you've already set foot in my territory?" I snarled, still needing to maintain my power.

"Fuck off, Tides. I told you, Creekwood is a border town."

"My border town, prick."

"What do you want?" he growled.

"I'll let you in, but only you and Raines. Since I know your cocks are attached."

"Why you—"

"Only the two of you, and once he's dead, you're out. You even think about bringing any men with you, and my men will kill each one."

Disconnecting, I sat back in my chair. I'd done something I'd never done, but Riley was more important to me than my pride. And with two bosses hunting him, Randall didn't stand a chance.

I spent the next hour digging back into numbers, leaving my office door open so I could listen for Riley. I had every one of my men but the two watching the house hunting for Randall. My instinct told me I should have put one or two on the road that led to Treemont, but I had invited Mason in and I knew he'd honor my demand to come with only Tyson. I would if I were in his place because the stakes were too high to take any chances. He wanted his sister, and he wanted Clint Randall dead, and I'd delivered both to him. If Mason didn't put him in a body bag, I would. Riley was an issue I'd have to deal with. With Mason hunting Randall, he'd find her and the truth would come out. I needed to tell her everything, to confess my sins and hope she forgave me. But I needed the man who threatened her safety dead first.

"I saw someone." Riley's voice drew my focus, and I saw her standing in the doorway. Strands of hair fell lazily against her face, bringing out the emerald of her eyes. The blouse she wore had loosened and the swell of her breast lay exposed, the sleeves falling past her wrists. There was a wounded look to her I wanted to fix.

I gave her the silence, hoping she would open up to me even as I saw the hypocrisy in that hope.

Rubbing her arm, she said, "Someone who hurt me." She dropped her eyes, staring at the floor as she spoke. "It happened almost a year ago. He...I thought I was in love. He lured me in, I fell for it, and he used me as revenge against my brother." Her eyes raised and the pain in them crushed me. I saw then the damage we all wreaked, running our territories with violence and revenge, using and hurting people for our own gain. It was something we overlooked, the uncomfortableness of it, the guilt buried away after years of dulling our emotions to it. But for someone like Riley, the reality of it was shattering.

She walked over to the window and looked out as she continued. "My brother fed me lies my entire life, never telling me who he was." Shit, that's why she'd left. She'd mentioned lies, but I hadn't realized it was to that extent. He'd left her in the dark and, in turn, hurt her when he'd only wanted to keep her protected. "This man used that, gaining my trust until he turned on me. He kidnapped me, beat me, and...tried to kill me when my brother found me."

I'd left my trail of bodies and damage over my years, but never had I wanted to kill someone like I wanted to kill Clint Randall. To make him suffer the way he'd made Riley suffer. I would let her watch as I shredded every ounce of life from him until I handed the knife to her and let her plunge it through what remained.

"As painful as his hands were when he hit me, as hurtful as his words were when he broke my heart, the thing that hurt the most while I laid in that hospital bed for days was how my brother had lied to me for so many years. Never trusting me enough to let me in, building a life for me and acting like I was building it on my own, letting me believe I was getting into the college of my dreams, that I was getting the dream job, that I was making something of myself." She turned, tears in her eyes, ones that gutted me. "When all that time I was doing none of it. It was all him protecting me. I never asked for his protection and look where it got me in the end."

Rising, I walked to her, taking her in my arms and holding her. I didn't know what to say, because everything Mason did was exactly what I would have done. It was what I was doing now—protecting her, setting her up with everything she needed to be happy because that's what I knew. That's what Mason knew.

I held her until the tension slipped from her body. "I won't let that man hurt you again, Riley. If he's in my city, I'll find him, and I promise you, I'll make him pay."

She snuggled deeper into my hold.

"I want you to stay with me until I find him."

"But I don't have clothes here—"

"I'll buy you clothes."

She pushed from me, the fire returning to her eyes. "You're not buying me more. You buy me too much. I'll stay, but I need some things from my apartment, and don't think this is me moving in with you."

"Stubborn woman," I grumbled. I needed her with me so I could protect her and moving in with me ensured she would always be in my grasp.

I took Riley to her apartment and stood guard as she packed her things. This wasn't the way I'd intended to have her move in with me, but this was how it would be. We were a few days from Christmas. I was hoping we'd have the asshole before then so she could have a relaxing day with me.

When we returned, I waited for her to unpack her clothes. Fingering the small box that held her final Christmas gift, I tucked it away to a more discreet spot so she wouldn't discover it until I was ready. I wasn't sure how she'd take the gift, but it felt right. Riley was mine, and I wouldn't let her go now that I had her. If it meant I'd have to deal with her brother, then so be it.

"You really have a lot of suits," she muttered, coming out of my closet. I glanced over at her. She'd changed into a pair of snug jeans that emphasized her pert ass and a low-cut t-shirt that made her neck almost too appealing not to kiss. I wanted to run my tongue along it, but I knew she was still nervous, and satisfying my desire for her wasn't the right thing to do.

"What?" she asked, pushing a strand of hair from her eyes.

"Nothing, just thinking of how perfect you are."

She beamed, her cheeks flushing. I held my hand out to her, intending to lead her downstairs and fix us some dinner while she sat by the fire. I couldn't help but give her a scolding look when she yanked me over to her.

She tipped her neck up to me, saying, "You look like you want to devour me, Mr. Tides."

Humor shone in her eyes, causing me to chuckle, and I dropped my lips to her neck just as I'd imagined doing. I pulled her against me, letting my hands trail her body. I could touch her every day for the rest of my life and never tire of it.

"Is this appropriate, Miss Brinks?" I asked, nibbling on her earlobe.

"I think it could be," she breathed.

My phone buzzed, and I tensed.

"Can't you ignore it this time, Grey?" she asked. And how I wanted to because making love to her was so much more tempting. But I wasn't about to take a chance of letting my guard down with her in danger.

"Not this time. Be a good girl and get in the bed and wait for me while I take this."

She giggled and ran to the bed, jumping on it as I looked at my phone. It was Den, so I knew it had to do with Randall. I'd sent every one of my men but a handful out to search the city for him.

"Speak," I said, walking toward the door.

"We found him."

My heart raced, and I stopped in my tracks, looking back at Riley. She'd worked her shirt off, her thin lace bra leaving nothing to my imagination.

"Fuck," I muttered. "Where?"

She must have seen my expression, her brow furrowing as she sat up and climbed from the bed.

"He's in a room in the Henly Hotel. We locked down the floor. There's nowhere for him to go."

"Are you sure?" I asked, knowing how adept the Bad Omen were at hiding.

"Yeah."

My phone buzzed again, a picture loading of a man who looked very close to the picture Mason had given me of Clint Randall. He wore a hat as if to conceal his identity, but there was no hiding the tattoo that marked him as an Omen. The bottom half of it showed just below his sleeve, embedded within a large spider design—the ugly black skull with the rusted dagger piercing it. Every Omen wore their brand in a different place. This one matched Randall's exactly.

"I'll be right there," I told Den. "Text me the room number."

"Grey?" Riley asked as I hung up.

"I need to go. I have something to take care of. When I get back, I'll explain everything."

"What's everything? What's going on, Greyson?"

She didn't know I knew anything about Clint Randall other than the minor details she'd shared, and I didn't have time to explain it now.

I took her face in my hands. "Trust me, please. I'll leave security outside the house. When I return, you'll be safe again and then no more secrets. I promise you."

Kissing her quickly, I rushed from the room, grabbing my jacket and the pistol I kept hidden close to it. I signaled for the two men watching the house to stay alert as I jumped in my car. With Randall in my grasp, Riley was safe, but I wasn't taking a chance.

I raced to the hotel in the center of the city and bolted up to the room, ready to enact justice on the fucker who had hurt Riley. I'd bring her his dead body and explain it all to her—the truth from start to finish—and hope she overlooked the fact that I was just like her brother. That she'd run from one mob boss to another, one web of lies to the next. Then I'd make her mine forever.

Den and several of my men stood outside, ready to pounce and awaiting my lead. I kicked the door in, and it splintered in half with the impact. This was my hotel, and the door was collateral damage that was easily repaired, unlike Riley's heart.

The thought of her loving him, of him touching her and fucking her, burned through me like a red-hot flame and I threw him against the wall, only then seeing that it wasn't him. There were striking similarities, but I'd ingrained the image of the bastard in my head, and this wasn't Clint Randall.

I punched him and pushed his shirt sleeve up, looking for the mark and finding it exactly where I'd seen it in both photos, but that didn't make sense. No other Omen would have their brand in that exact place. They strategically placed each one in a unique spot so there was no pattern to where they were, and they went undetected by most.

"Where the fuck is Randall?" I growled, putting my gun to his temple.

"He said to tell you he's playing with your pretty thing," he said. There was a nervous shake to his voice, one no Omen would have. I grabbed his arm again, rubbing the tattoo, which smudged with a small amount of pressure.

"Fuck, he's a mark," Den said, meeting my eyes.

Marks were people desperate enough to sell their soul to a family for something they needed. Whether it was money, protection for a loved one, medicine for a sick child, they forfeited their lives, the family paying out their wish once their deed was done. The families rarely used them unless they needed a sacrifice, a distraction from a crime, or in this case, from a target. Randall had found a mark who was close enough in appearance to fool even me—a change of hair color, a few days of facial hair, and we didn't notice from a distance. That explained the lethal mistake my men had made. The same I'd made by leaving Riley alone.

I knocked the mark out with the blunt end of my gun and glared at Den. "Dispose of him, and then you can explain why you fell for their trap after I kill the fucker."

"But boss—"

"Just do it!"

I didn't wait for a reply, running out of the hotel and tearing back to my house. I should have brought men with me, but my mind was only on Riley. My heart was pounding so hard I could barely breathe. Images of Riley in fear, of her hurt, of her dead invaded my mind. I'd promised she was safe, and I'd left her to the wolves.

Not bothering to turn my car off, I drew my gun, running into the house. I found one of my men down with a gunshot to his head in the foyer. I didn't have to question if Randall had taken the other out.

"Fuck!" I rounded the stairs, seeing where the struggle had taken place. Riley had run to the bedroom and tried to shut herself in, but he'd broken through. I stood in the center of the scene, spotting the splatter of blood on my bed sheets as if he'd hit her hard enough for the blood to travel.

My world came crumbling down, and I grasped at where to find her. She was out there with an enemy. One who would use her to crush both me and Mason because he knew how valuable she was to both of us.

I searched the rest of the house, running out the back to find the bloodstained snow where my second man had fallen prey to Clint's gun.

"Fuck!" I screamed.

Running to the front of the house, I stopped and scolded myself for letting my emotions take over my rational thinking. Riley was smart. She was Mason Brinks' sister, and even if he hadn't included her in the life he led, she was calculating like he was. She had run from him, hiding her tracks so even he couldn't find her. That said something about her.

I ran back into the house and to the room, looking for clues. Someone had violently removed the lamp from the wall, and it was on the floor on the other side of the room. Riley had used it to defend herself. I scanned where she'd been unpacking her things, remembering how she'd dropped her phone and keys on the dresser.

I searched, finding the keys but not the phone. Taking my phone out, I held my breath, pulling up the tracker I had on hers.

"Good girl," I muttered, seeing the mark that was moving quickly through town. She'd snuck her phone somehow, and now I had a way to find her.

I bolted back to my car, driving faster than I should have on the icy roads. My only thought was getting to Riley before the bastard hurt her more.

Chapter Twenty

RILEY

The soft lights in Greyson's kitchen were calming as I waited for my tea to brew. I wished he'd stayed and ignored the call. There was something he wanted to tell me. I could see it in his eyes when he told me he'd be back soon. A shadow passed over the back window and my nerves heightened. I backed away, hoping it was just an animal. I was on edge, and every noise and movement made me jumpy. Seeing Clint earlier had left me unsure and shaken. I was debating calling Mason and giving up my attempt at independence from him just so he could protect me again. Not that I thought Greyson wouldn't try. He was strong and capable, with plenty of security. But he didn't run in the same world as Clint Randall or my brother.

The front door opened, and I turned, expecting to see Greyson, but a burly blonde man entered, bringing his finger to his mouth. Instinctively, I screamed, stumbling back. He shook his head, drawing a gun from his jacket, and I remembered Greyson's security team was outside the house. I would have calmed some, but for the worry in the man's eyes.

"Riley, I work for Greyson. There's someone in the house. I need you to—"

He didn't finish, his eyes going blank as a gun went off and his brains splattered across the wall. Another scream tore from me, and I backed into the counter. Fear seized me so that I couldn't move.

"Did you miss me, baby?" Clint's eyes were beady like an animal's as he slipped his gun in his jacket. "You've been a busy girl, fucking your way into Greyson Tides' bed. I didn't see that one coming. Not only will you bring me Brinks, but I'll break Tides with him. Two for one."

He walked closer, and my instincts kicked in. I eyed the stairs. He was blocking the front door, and the sliding doors were too far from where I stood. The stairs were close, and I dashed for them, but Clint grabbed my ankle. I hit the bottom stair hard, crying out from the impact. Pain shot through my arm that had taken the force of the fall. Ignoring it, I kicked my foot, connecting with Clint's jaw, and heard him grumble as I scrambled up the stairs.

"You can't run from me, baby. I'm gonna ruin you for Tides and send your body to him after I lure your brother here and kill him."

I didn't understand why he was talking about Greyson like he knew him, putting him in the same context as Mason, but I didn't have time to contemplate it. Slamming the bedroom door behind me, I fumbled with the lock and backed up, looking for anything I could use as a weapon. I was too far up and only then did I realize how dumb I'd been to corner myself here. I needed to call Mason, to tell him Clint was here. To have him save me. I grabbed my cell phone, remembering that Mason couldn't track it. I could have called Greyson, but he didn't know how dangerous Clint was, and I didn't want him hurt. Mason would find me and rescue me again. It never occurred to me that he was too far away and there was no way he could make it there in time. Tucking my new phone down my shirt, I rummaged through my bag and found my other phone. As I waited for it to power up, Clint's fists pounded on the door, making me jump. My heart was racing, my entire body shaking so hard I could barely hold the phone.

"Come out and play, Riley. I miss the feel of those lips around my cock, baby. I'm gonna fuck you so hard you'll beg me to stop until I cover your body with my cum." My stomach turned, his words making me sick. He'd always been foul-mouthed and vulgar with his comments about sex. At the time, I'd found it sexy because it opposed everything Mason would have wanted me to like in a man. Clint had offered me an outlet to rebel, and I'd taken it without ever seeing the risk. "I want Mason to know that I had you again before I execute him. Maybe I'll take a picture and send it to Tides. Fuck, that sounds perfect."

His vile suggestion reminded me of all the times I'd let him touch me, enjoying it and believing he loved me. He'd always been a brutal lover, taking me hard and fast, never caring to satisfy me unless it was something he wanted. So I didn't doubt that he'd do just what he was threatening before he killed me. I stared at the phone impatiently, waiting for it to load. I was running on adrenaline, my eyes searching the room for anything to defend myself with. Grabbing the lamp, I yanked the cord from the wall, the table falling over with the force. The phone powered, and I quickly put the tracker on, then called Mason just as Clint started kicking the door in.

"Ri—"

"Mason, he's here—"

The door shattered, and I hastily stuffed the phone in the back of my pants, praying Clint wouldn't find it. He was threatening to fuck me, so there was a high probability he would. I didn't know what I was thinking, taking the time to call Mason, but hearing his voice strengthened me. He may have sheltered me, but I was his sister. I may have been nine years younger, but that didn't mean I hadn't observed him all that time. Maybe I missed the signs that should have told me he was involved in more than real estate, but I observed the way he carried himself and the way he and Tyson would box in the backyard. The two of them had been my world.

I held the lamp out like a baseball bat, ready to hit Clint with it.

"That's cute, Riley. Do you really think you can fight me? Sheltered, naïve Riley Brinks. How did you end up in the bed of the most notorious mob boss in the territories? Too blind to notice your brother's lies, and you turn around and fall for another man's?"

His words threw me off guard, and he seized the opportunity, rushing me as I swung the lamp too late. He caught it and pushed me to the bed, his large body encasing mine. I fought, scratching at him, but he pulled me up by my hair, his laugh vicious and cruel. My fist connected with his chin, but the move only stopped his laugh, his mouth tightening in irritation. He raised his hand, smacking me so hard my lip split, and blood filled my mouth.

Yanking me toward him, he sneered. "You're a stupid whore. I'm gonna have fun breaking your heart again. I want to see you wilt when I tell you more truths, because watching you break that way is almost as good as watching you come."

He smacked me again and the blood that had pooled in my mouth splattered across the bed. I pushed at him to get away, but he was too strong and my adrenaline had fled, leaving me exhausted.

Pulling his gun out, he held it to my temple, saying, "Stop fighting or I'll kill you now and fuck your dead body over Tides' bed. He can explain to your brother why the blood and cum soaked body of his sister is in his bed. That should start a nice territory war. It's a tempting thought, but I need to break you more. I'm supposed to send you back to my boss. See, at first, he planned to sell your sexy little body to whoever offered him the most money, but now he's particularly interested in meeting the whore who seduced Greyson Tides. But I'm going to have some fun with you first and if I kill you while I do, I'll just blame it on that fucker Tides. Walk, or I shoot, and Tides has no chance to save you with his lies."

He pushed me forward, grabbing my wrists and forcing me out of the room. My mind was trying to make sense of his words, of the idea that Greyson was somehow involved in the same things my brother was. It didn't make sense, but Clint talked about him as if he knew him, as if everyone knew him. It couldn't be. Just like none of this could be happening. Maybe I'd slipped on the stairs and knocked myself out. Maybe I'd wake up in Greyson's bed with a concussion and find him sitting beside me, waiting worriedly for me to wake.

Clint shoved me into his car and drove off, his wheels screeching on the snowy pavement. My heart was thudding, and I wanted to cry. I didn't know how to escape this time. I'd only escaped last time because Mason had saved me. But he wasn't here. He wouldn't save me.

"You are amazing, Riley. How, after all the sobbing and whining you did when I told you the truth about your brother, did you fall for Greyson Tides? He's an old man, baby. You had my cock, and that's what you turn to?"

"Fuck you, Clint. He's not old, and his cock is bigger than yours."

"Maybe you just have a type. Is that what it is?" he continued. "A bad guy thing? Are you looking for your brother in every dick you suck?"

I grabbed the wheel and jerked it, sending the car spinning on the ice. Clint was swearing as he tried to gain control. I fumbled for my seatbelt, trying to buckle it, but we slid, gaining speed and careening into a jewelry store, glass splattering everywhere as the tail of the car took the store display out. The car halted with a force that knocked the wind from me, and my head hit the dashboard. Stars clouded my vision, pain shooting through my head. It took me a minute to lift it and look over at Clint. He was holding his nose, which was gushing blood.

"You bitch, you broke my nose," he growled.

I tried to get out of the car, but the crash had jammed my door. The window had shattered with the impact, and I crawled out, hope blooming that I might just have a chance. Clint's grasp on my ankle shattered that hope, but I fought, kicking at him until he released me. I hoisted myself further until I was out, wobbling when my feet touched the ground. My head pounded, my vision blurring before it focused. Forcing myself to run, I could hear Clint curse at me as he freed himself from the car. My phone had fallen from my pants in my rush, but I still had my other one and I pulled it out, trying to figure out where I was. There was only one person left to call. I hit Greyson's number.

"You can't run, Riley! You can never escape me!"

Greyson answered on the first ring. "Riley!"

"Help me. He's going to kill me."

"Fuck. I'm on my way."

I skidded to a stop as I rounded a corner, a snowbank in front of me. He'd driven me to the far side of town where the older businesses were. The nightlife was on the other end. This part of town closed down at sunset. There was no one to help me, no one to hear me scream.

"Riley!" Greyson yelled into the phone.

Clint tackled me, sending the phone flying from my hand. I screamed as he shoved my face into the snow. Terror as sharp as a knife whipped through me and I struggled to breathe. Flailing wildly, I tried to free myself. When I was close to blacking out, Clint let me go, climbing off me and dragging me by my arm to my phone.

Picking it up, he calmly said, "Greyson Tides."

I could hear Greyson on the other end. He'd stopped yelling, his voice terse and cold, but I couldn't make out his words.

"What does it take to break a man like you, Tides? Maybe I'll watch as you find her pretty face bloodied and wearing my cum.

Should I send a piece of her to her brother? Maybe carve my initials in her delicate skin so he knows who fucked her last?"

I could hear Greyson now. The calm in his voice had disappeared.

Clint snapped my body back, pinning me against his chest. "What do you think, baby? You wanna take my cock once more? Should I let old Greyson listen?"

I whimpered, trying to stand as my legs gave out.

"Say goodbye to him, Riley."

He put the phone to my ear. "Grey—"

"Riley, I'm almost there. Get away if you can. I promise you he won't hurt you anymore and I will let you watch as I fucking gut him."

"Enough of that dirty talk, Tides. I'll be sure to let you hear her take her last breath. Oh, and Tides, your brother sends his love."

He threw the phone and yanked me close to him, holding the gun to my head. "Let's have a talk before your old man gets here. I want to watch your face as I destroy you more, you pathetic bitch."

"I hate you. I hope Mason hunts you down and kills you."

"Mason? Not Greyson? Huh, their names rhyme. You have a brother fetish, baby?"

I spit a mouthful of blood at him, and he backhanded me. Wiping his face, he yanked me back up. His eyes were dark, and I wondered if he'd just kill me then.

"Let's talk about your old man and how naïve you are. Greyson Tides, the most notorious of all the bosses. Your brother thought he'd step into Greyson's territory, but Tides isn't someone to fuck with, and he's been at this a lot longer. And with that move, they became enemies. What do you think happened when the pretty little sister of Mason Brinks moved to Greyson's city?"

I tried backing away, not wanting to hear anymore, a painful burning building in my chest.

"Well, Tides plays a slow game, baby. He lured you into his trap, and you fell head first, as usual. You're so easy to play. You'd think you would have learned from me, but you went and did it again."

"No, he didn't. That can't be. He loves me."

"Love? Tides? Oh baby, Tides loves nothing but power. You were the prey in his hunt." My fight left me, those words slamming into me like a vicious storm. They were the exact words Greyson had said to me. That I was his prey. "Did you know the perv even had a camera installed in your apartment? He watched you through the apartment next door. I saw him leave one night and broke in. Nice set-up and a fantastic view of your room, your bed, your body. Fuck, I wish I'd been that clever. But then again, you willingly spread your legs for me right away."

I didn't know what to say. Everything Clint had said left me in shock and my mind was filling in all the blanks, confirming it was the truth. The way Greyson had snuck into my apartment, leaving me gifts, knowing when I was asleep. Pain more intense than my wounds stabbed at my heart.

"That's it, Riley. I love watching you break."

A car screeched into the lot, and Clint turned me, using me as a shield, my back pinned to his chest, his gun to my head.

Greyson stepped out of the car, powerful and beautiful. No fear lined his face, only a lethal hardness that sat in his blue eyes.

"Drop the gun, Randall."

"Oh, but Tides, Riley and I have been catching up, haven't we, baby?"

"You fucking call her baby again and I'll slit your throat just enough for you to feel every ounce of pain I give the rest of your body."

"I was calling her baby long before your cock was pounding into her."

Greyson growled, a sound that usually would have had me soaked, but I wasn't sure how to feel now. I had a gun to my head and a dagger in my heart.

"Do you want to finish filling her in on how you were using her to get to Brinks? Or should I continue?"

Greyson's face dropped, confirming everything Clint had said.

"Ah, Tides. Time to destroy you completely. Because she hates you now. She knows the truth and she'll die hating you, not loving you like you wanted. Too bad I'll be the one taking Brinks down and—"

What happened next was so fast, I wasn't sure how it had happened. Greyson pulled his gun so quickly that Clint hadn't even finished his last word before the shot went off, hitting him between the eyes. He fell back as I recoiled from the sound. Greyson ran toward me, but I stumbled away. He stopped, his eyes so wounded it hurt me even more.

I stood across from him with Clint dead at my feet, unsure of my next move and feeling like my life had fractured so severely that I might never piece it back together this time.

I didn't know fear, but the moment I knew Clint Randall had Riley, I understood fear like it was a close friend. It raked through me, piercing my chest with a pain that pounded through it. And with every passing minute, it increased, closing in on me like a snake constricting my lungs.

I was driving too fast, but I didn't care. My need to get to Riley had taken over all others. I glanced at my phone as I ran another red light. The mark that signified her location had stopped moving, and my heart jumped to my throat. There were only two reasons the location would be static: Randall had found the phone, or he was getting ready to kill her. I was so close to the location, but I was still too far, and my chest was so tight it was difficult to breathe. I clutched the steering wheel, running every red light.

My phone rang, Riley's number coming up, and fear gripped me further.

"Riley!"

"Help me. He's going to kill me." The terror in her voice crushed me, and I bit back the emotion.

"Fuck. I'm on my way."

There was silence, and my fear twisted like a knife blade.

"Riley!"

"Greyson Tides." Clint Randall's voice was calm. He had the power, and he knew it.

"You touch a fucking hair on her head, and I will ensure your death is slow and painful."

A slew of vile words came at me, shredding my calm, and I roared, "I will hunt you down like the piece of shit you are, Randall. Walk away now or you'll be begging me for mercy!"

He didn't respond. Instead, he threatened Riley, my blood boiling more with each word he spewed. I heard her whimper and my heart wrenched. I was so close to the west end of town where they were.

"Grey—" Riley's voice came through the phone again, further eviscerating my heart with its desperation.

I tried to reassure her, promising that I would kill him, but Randall must have snatched the phone from her again. His smug words twisted at my need to slaughter him, his last statement like the venomous strike of a cobra.

The phone disconnected, and I punched the steering wheel. My brother. The head of the Bad Omens. The thorn in my thigh. We'd stayed away from each other, kept in our territories for decades after our falling out, but now he'd crossed the line. First by having Clint Randall infiltrate Mason, then when Randall stumbled into my territory following Riley. And now the prick had leverage on me—he had Riley, and if Randall had been watching her this entire time, he'd know she was mine. But my brother was too much like me, and there was no way he would kill Riley if he knew she belonged to me. He would have Randall deliver her to him. He'd use her and crush her even further. If he decided not to keep her, he'd sell her to the highest bidder and send me the receipt before he made his move to take me down. That meant Randall was either a good bullshitter or a deserter who was turning on my brother. Someone that foolish was an even greater risk than I had anticipated because it meant he was unhinged and untethered to any laws of his family.

I turned past a car that had slammed into the jewelry store where my shop was. But Riley wasn't there. The phone was showing her around the corner, and I knew she must have run from him when they crashed.

"That's my girl," I mumbled as I tore around the corner, screeching to a halt and jumping from the car. Randall jerked Riley to him, his gun to her head.

She was bloody and looked exhausted. Seeing her like that was devastating, and it took every ounce of strength not to let the pain of it show. What was even more devastating was the hurt in her eyes.

Clint spewed his macho words, but the ones that hit their mark were the ones about how he'd told her everything. And I could see it in her eyes, the anguish in them wrecking me completely. I had wanted to explain it all to her. I had planned to once I eliminated the threat, but he'd beaten me to it, using the truth to hurt her more than the wounds had.

As he rambled, I saw my opening and took it, shooting him in the head. Riley's scream cut me as his body fell to the ground. I'd wanted to torture the son of a bitch more now than I ever had, but I needed Riley safe. I stepped toward her, but she backed away, fracturing me with the fear and distrust that lined her eyes.

"Riley, I—"

"Is it true?" she asked, her voice quivering. "Is everything true? Did you lure me here? Use me to get back at Mason?"

"I..."

"No more lies, Greyson."

I didn't want to talk about this. I needed to get her to a hospital to have the wound on her head looked at, and the cuts and bruises soothed.

"Dammit, Greyson, tell me."

"Yes, but only at first."

Her face dropped.

"Riley, I need—"

"You need? Why is it the men in my life always need something without ever thinking of what I need? I needed the truth, Greyson. I needed..." Her lips trembled, and the sight left my heart riven. The sob she stifled shredded me. "I needed you to be something else, something different. But you're not. You're just like them."

Tires screeched, and a car rounded the corner, its speed too fast. I rushed to Riley and threw her behind me against her complaints. Drawing my gun, I readied myself to protect her, cursing myself for fleeing without my men. I'd hear an earful from Den when this was over, after I finished chewing him out about the mark.

"Step away from my sister!" Mason screamed, jumping from the car, guns drawn. Tyson hopped from the passenger seat, his gun out. "Get away from her, Tides!" Mason ordered me. The flippant little shit. I should have shot him. I'd let him into my city, but he'd been in my territory before I'd called him. That gave me every right to splatter the ground with his blood, regardless of our agreement. I would have killed both him and Tyson, if not for Riley. "Riley, come here, now."

She stepped from behind me, pushing my arm from her. Mason glanced down at Clint Randall's body, then back at me.

"I told you I'd give you his dead body, Brinks," I said, my eyes dropping to Riley. "I won't hurt her."

"No? You fucking knew she was in your city this entire time, didn't you? And you didn't bother telling me? I knew I couldn't trust you, fucking lying to me this entire time. Get the fuck over here, Riley, and away from him. You think I'm bad? Tides takes the crown on bad."

Her eyes met mine, the doubt sealed with those words.

"Riley, please," I said, hating that it sounded like I was

begging. Because I was. The thought of being away from her was devastating. It was like drowning with no way back to the surface.

"You hurt me, Greyson. You lied to me...you..."

"Did you touch my sister, Tides?"

"Fuck off, Brinks. This isn't your business."

Tyson shifted closer. "Not our business? She's covered in blood!" he said.

"From the asshole you let in your ranks, then let close to her. That shit wouldn't have happened on my watch."

"No? Looks like he got to her after we made our deal and while you were on watch," Mason said. "Riley." He held his hand out, and she walked to him, taking it. Mason gestured to Tyson to drive and opened the door for her, his gun still on me.

"Riley, don't do this," I said, my chest berated with pain like I'd never experienced. I lowered my gun as Mason climbed into the seat next to her. She leaned into him, and Tyson tore from the lot. I stood there, feeling as if part of my soul had been gauged from my body. The ache in my chest was almost too much to handle.

I didn't know how long I stood there, my eyes on the spot where she had been, before I finally put my gun away and took my phone out. Hardening myself to the pain, I called Den.

"I need clean up behind Frank's, and there's a car through his window. Take care of it and get someone to fix the damage."

I hung up before he could respond and walked back to my car, knowing there was nothing to do but bury myself back in my work, pretending Riley Brinks had never entered my city or my life. Removing the traces of her until she faded from my heart like the essence of a spirit long gone. I didn't know if that was possible, but I had no choice but to believe it was. Thinking otherwise would be akin to dying. Although I felt like I'd died, my heart ripped from my chest and riddled with a thousand bullets.

Sobs rocked my body so hard I thought it would splinter into a thousand pieces. Mason held me tight, and I could feel the tension, the worry that sat in his frame. I didn't think the agony that was wrenching my heart, severing it until there was nothing left, would ever fade. The truth of Greyson's life and the lies on which our love had sat so precariously gnawed away at the fragments that were holding me together.

Mason rubbed my back, his hand coming up to run over my hair as he kissed my head. As much of an ass as he could be, he had always been my rock and, in that moment, he was the only thing keeping me together.

"Ri…" I buried my face further into his chest, not wanting to talk. The ache was too raw, and I wasn't sure if it would ever heal. I felt like Greyson had ripped out my heart and ravaged it after I'd handed it to him, trusting that he'd protect it, that he loved me just as much as I loved him. The truth was something I should have seen. The clues had been there, in plain sight. The sneaking into my apartment, the stalking, the key he had…all signs I chose not to see as anything more than an obsession that was driven by the attraction and love he had for me. But it hadn't been. It had been driven by revenge against Mason and a need to use me. To devastate me and lure my brother to his death.

He was no different from Clint Randall. That pain had been nothing but a dull ache compared to this. What Greyson had done had left me wounded to the core, my soul damaged, my heart mangled.

Another sob tore its way through my body before it broke free, loud and ugly.

"Shit, Mace. Is she okay?" I heard Tyson ask from the front of the car.

"I don't know," Mason answered, and I could hear the pain in his voice. I had hurt him, run from him and his protection, and now he was rescuing me again. Left picking up the pieces from my mistakes. Only this time, I didn't think he could put them back together.

"Ri, please tell me you didn't fall in love with Greyson Tides," he said, trying to lift my face.

I couldn't answer. Couldn't admit that I had and that I'd handed him my heart, not knowing the disastrous effect he would have on it. Not expecting the consequences. Even in the short time he'd held it.

"Dammit, Riley. Tides is my enemy, and you walked right into his trap." Another rupture splintered my heart, sending more tears soaking Mason's shirt. "Why would you go to Bridgeville? Of all the places to run. Fuck, I should turn around and kill him."

"Want me to, Mace?" Tyson asked. But I gripped Mason's shirt, picking my head up and meeting his green eyes. The worry that sat in them, mixed with the hurt that remained from the damage I'd done when I left him, only added to my agony.

"No," I choked out between the tears.

Mason brought his thumb up to brush them away. "Why not? He hurt you, Ri. He..." His eyes darkened, his jaw tightening below the stubble that sat upon it. "He fucking touched you. Just like that asshole Randall. He used you and you...dammit, Ri. Why did you run? Why couldn't you have just stayed with me? I could have protected you."

I didn't need his anger or his lectures and I tried to turn away from him, but he grabbed my chin, forcing me to look at him.

"Let up on her, Mace," Tyson said. "She's not in the condition for you to guilt her. Let's just get her home."

My love for Tyson increased with his support. He'd always been like a second brother to me, but it was usually Mason who kept him in check.

Mason's features softened, his eyes looking for something in mine, answers I couldn't give him. Explanations and apologies I owed him but couldn't provide because Greyson had left me too damaged to even try.

"Did you fall in love with him, Ri?" he asked again.

More tears fell, his words like a knife shredding what remained of the strands that were holding my heart together. I nodded, my chest so tight with the sob I was restraining that it was agony.

"Fuck," he said.

"I thought..." I started, my cry coming out so raw it burned my throat.

Mason pulled me back into his chest, his arms so tight around me that it was like he never wanted to let me go. I held onto his shirt, my tears a waterfall that wouldn't stop. My external injuries were minor this time compared to when Clint had hurt me, but my inner wounds were ones I doubted would ever heal. They riddled my soul and my heart so badly that there was no repairing them.

Mason didn't say any more, and I let him be my strength, knowing I had none left. What strength I'd had was on the ground of that parking lot with the body of Clint Randall and the shards of my heart.

THE SNOW FELL in large flakes, floating like tiny ghosts in the hazy sky beyond my window. Christmas had come and gone, the usual joy of the season buried below my pain and tears. Mason tried convincing me to forget Greyson, but it was too hard. He was in my mind, in my heart, in my soul, no matter that he'd hurt me. It would take years to erase his touch from my body.

Mason checked on me often, but I ignored him, staring out my window each time and rarely leaving the guest room he'd settled me in. I barely touched the food he brought me, barely slept, my dreams haunted by Clint and that night. Haunted by the truth of who Greyson really was, the truth of what he'd done and how he'd used me just like Clint had. Each time I thought about it, the pain grew because as much as I'd thought I loved Clint, it was nothing to what I felt for Greyson. That had been infatuation, lust, but this...this was love—the soul shattering, heart wrenching, never completely healing kind.

"Ri?" Mason's voice came around my door as I heard him open it. I didn't know how long I'd been there. The days seemed to blur. I vaguely remembered hearing Mason whisper happy New Year through the door to me one night, but I may have imagined it.

I heard him enter my room, expecting he'd drop a tray of food off and make small talk I wouldn't take part in. "Greyson is here."

Hearing Greyson's name brought the pain to the surface. I didn't know how to react to Mason's words. He hated Greyson, so it made little sense that he'd let Greyson anywhere near me.

"Ri, it's been a month. Talk to him."

I turned my eyes to him. It was the first time I'd looked at him since the night he'd held me in the back of his car as my tears had fallen. My bruises had healed since then. The small scar on my forehead was the only reminder of that night besides the constant ache in my chest.

"Why would you want me to talk to him?" My voice sounded raw, and I didn't think I'd spoken since that night, listening as Mason told me about Greyson and their rivalry. Listening as the nurses patched me up and wiped away the blood like I wanted them to wipe away the pain.

"Because I love you more than my pride. I don't know what to do to help you, Ri. There isn't much I can't fix, and you won't let me fix you. This isn't anything like what happened with Clint. You got over that, even if you continued to give me the silent treatment. But this.... I've never seen you like this. And as much as I hate Tides, I think the asshole is as hurt as you are."

I scrunched my brows, wondering how that could be. "He used me, Mason."

"He's not Clint Randall, Riley. If he were using you, he would have killed you the night he took Clint out. At least hear him out. Or at least tell him to fuck off and get angry at him. I hate seeing you like this. It's like you're broken."

Because I was. Broken was exactly how I felt. Shattered like a piece of glass under the weight of a heavy load, fractured into tiny fragments. I rose, pulling my sweater around me, and walked past Mason, not saying anything further. Maybe I needed to face Greyson, if only to get past the tears and the raw pain that wouldn't heal.

I saw him standing at the gates, waiting for me, the snow dropping on his black coat and in his auburn hair. I pulled my boots on and walked out, the cold seeping below my wool cardigan. Feeling something other than sorrow was nice, and I embraced it.

Greyson looked up as the gates opened, and I stood just beyond them, not getting close. His brow furrowed, his eyes taking me in with sadness. I was sure I looked a mess. I didn't know if I'd showered or even combed my hair in days. The sleepless nights had surely left dark circles under my eyes, and I'd lost weight from eating so little.

"What is it, Greyson?" My voice was hollow, and I didn't recognize it.

"Riley, I'm sorry. I needed to tell you that. To explain everything like I planned to that night."

"Were you going to explain it? Or were you planning to keep me in your web of lies?"

"They weren't lies. None of them were."

"You didn't spy on me? You didn't have cameras watching me? You didn't plan to use me as revenge against my brother?"

He flinched at each word, and I noted how the powerful man I knew wasn't there. Greyson had come to me with vulnerability, and I didn't know what to make of it.

"I'm guilty of all of it. I lured you into my firm and away from the smaller firm. I set you up with your apartment. I wanted to get back at Mason, and yes, I planned to use you just like Randall did."

I couldn't stop the sob his words caused because hearing him say them aloud hurt worse than hearing them in my head.

"But that changed. The moment I saw you on the street that day. And every moment after. I didn't lie about how I feel about you, Riley. I love you, and no matter what happens, that won't ever change."

The tears burned, but I bit my lip, not wanting him to see them, not wanting him to see that his words were weaving their way into my soul.

"Please, Riley. I can't take it back, but I would give it all up for you."

"Give it all up? Your money? Your business? Your life? I doubt that Greyson." I rubbed my arms as the cold began to burn my limbs.

"I would. All of it."

"And who would you be without it? Who, Greyson? Because

it's part of you. It's not something you can give up so easily because who would that make you?"

He didn't respond, his face falling. I could see the defeat in his shoulders.

"I can't compete with your world, Greyson. It's not someplace I can live. Go back to Bridgeville."

I turned from him, the action opening the wounds further and hurting so much that I had to hold my arms for fear I would double over in pain. I didn't look back, and as I closed the door to the house, I heard him drive away.

Chapter Twenty-Three

GREYSON

The road passed by without my notice, my thoughts consumed by Riley just as they had been since the day I'd lost her. I'd foolishly gone to Treemont, risking Mason's wrath. And he'd let me talk to her, threatening to shoot me if I hurt her more and saying the only reason he wasn't killing me was that I'd taken Randall out. I didn't know what I was doing. Never had I been as desperate as I was to see her, as lost as I was without her.

Seeing her had only deepened the gutting pain that I'd carried since that night. The hollow, eviscerated feeling that sat in my chest. I'd tried forgetting her, tried burying myself in my work, but reminders of her were everywhere. The impression she'd left on my soul was one I couldn't rid myself of and I didn't know if I wanted to be rid of it. I loved her and I knew there would never be another I would love like I loved Riley.

Watching her walk down the path from Mason's house, her thin body lost in the thick cardigan she wore, had sent nerves stabbing their way through my body, igniting the agony that had berated my chest daily. But when she'd come closer, the sight of her had sent the ache spiraling uncontrollably. I thought seeing her would help, but it had only worsened the pain. Her appearance had burned through me like a hot iron, scorching me. She'd looked so thin, her eyes hollow and lined with circles, the same ones that lined my own from the sleepless nights of being without her. Her beautiful ebony hair was messy and knotted and seeing her like that only brought the guilt back to the surface. I'd done this to her, breaking her just like I'd originally wanted. But I didn't want this now. I wanted her whole and vibrant, her smile lighting my heart, her eyes shining like emeralds. But I'd fractured her, and I couldn't undo that, no matter what I said or did.

There was nothing I could do to take it back. My words had meant nothing to her, and she'd turned her back on me, leaving me there with only regrets and a sense of loss that threatened to drown me.

I drove straight through, not bothering to stop and rest. It wouldn't have helped. Sleep only slipped through my fingers now, like Riley had. I spotted Den behind me as I crossed into my territory. He would give me a lashing for leaving him behind, but I knew Mason wouldn't let me near Riley if I had any of my men with me. It had been risky, but I was so hollow at this point, death might have been a blessing.

Walking into my house, I heard Den catch up to me. I stood in the foyer, the same sensation of loss that hit me each time sinking into me. Everywhere I looked, I could see Riley. She hadn't been to my place more than a few times, but it didn't matter. I could see her snuggled up on my couch, the firelight dancing in her hair. Hear her giggle as I picked her up and carried her to the bed, feel her skin against mine, the warmth of her breath, the smell of her perfume...she was everywhere.

Den's hand came to my shoulder, bringing me out of the memories.

"I won't beat you up this time. I think you've done enough of that yourself," he said.

I glanced at him, trying to summon the energy to walk into

the house. He gave me an understanding look and walked further into the house, making his way to the kitchen where he fixed two glasses of scotch. Bringing one back to me, he said, "Do I need to ask where you went?"

"Probably not," I said, finally forcing myself to move.

I avoided the couch and the kitchen, going straight into my office, where I spent most of my time now. The rest of the house held too many memories.

"Dammit, Greyson. Brinks could have killed you—"

"You said you wouldn't beat me up for it," I said, rolling my neck and burying the defeat that sat heavy in my chest like the never-fading ache.

"I can't help it. Don't pull that shit again or I won't be here when you return."

I narrowed my eyes. "Is that a threat?"

"No, it's a promise. Do you have any idea how worried I was?" He took his phone from his pocket, shaking it in front of me. "How many texts I sent? How many unanswered calls before I figured out where your ass had gone?"

I threw my phone on the desk and sat, only then noticing all the missed calls. Running my hands through my hair, I leaned my head in them.

"Fuck, Greyson. You need to give her up. You did your damage—"

I brought my fists down on the desk, the sound echoing through the room.

"I didn't want to do damage," I growled.

"Yes, you did. Break and destroy. That's what this was. That's all it ever was."

"No..." I said, turning my eyes to the window, seeing the wind blow flurries around from the dusting we'd had overnight. "That's not all it ever was. That's how it started. But that's not how it ended."

He remained quiet for a few moments before he said, "We've

known each other a long time, Greyson, so I'm going to be honest. You need to let her go. The game is over, and you lost, she lost, even Brinks lost. I've never seen you this bad, but if any of your enemies see you this way, they'll know you're vulnerable."

I looked back at him, knowing he was right. It had been weeks, and I couldn't seem to climb from under the weight of knowing I'd lost Riley. Maybe it was time I tried again.

I SAT on the bed in Riley's apartment. The fairy lights cast a calming golden light over the room as I embraced the memories of her. I'd been thinking about her question—what would I be if I gave it all up? I hadn't known how to answer that question, but now that I'd had time to think about it, I knew the answer.

I fingered the ring I'd bought her right before Christmas, my intent to make her mine completely. Right before life had turned into a nightmare I couldn't escape. The diamond sparkled in the dim lighting as I thought about her question.

Riley had worked her way into my heart, finding a way in where no one ever had and even if I had to give it all up, having her would make it okay. She completed me and made me whole when I'd never known I was anything but that. Even after the short time she'd been in my life, I knew that with certainty, a clarity I'd never had. If I were no longer the power figure, the boss of the network I'd built, no longer the mogul who owned this part of the province, I would still be something. I would be hers.

Standing, I slipped the ring back into its box. I looked around the apartment once more. The movers would be packing it up in the morning with instructions to send it back to Riley. There was no need to keep it any longer. She wasn't coming back. I walked to her bed. The handful of scarves that had given me my first taste of her were still hanging there. I slid my fingers over the silk, pulling the red scarf out and bringing it to my nose. The smell of her lotion and perfume tickled my senses, threatening to tear down the barriers I was erecting around my heart. I put the scarf in my pocket, spying the blindfold on her nightstand. Smiling at the memory of lifting it the night she'd challenged me, I put it in my other pocket, knowing I couldn't give up every piece of her, no matter how much I convinced myself I needed to.

Walking back to the table, I placed the ring box into a larger box, the tissue paper below making a soft crinkle sound. I laid my answer to her question on top of the box, then sealed the larger box, brushing my fingers over the label with Riley's name and address. It was one last attempt to win her back, one I had little faith in, but I needed her to know the truth. To know that she'd worked her way into my heart where I hadn't thought anyone could reach. That she'd destroyed my plans, taking my game and twisting it into something more, something longer, something deeper.

With one last look at her apartment, I took the box and walked out, leaving my key along with the memories and past that had left more scars on me than any bullet ever had.

Chapter Twenty-Four

RILEY

Days passed, and I couldn't remove the sight of Greyson's pained expression from my mind. Mason had been away for a few days, and Tyson watched over me. He'd skipped bringing me dinner, so I wandered to the kitchen, noting how empty it was. Usually, Mason's men were in and out, but tonight it was quiet. An opened box sat on the island, and I saw a note nestled within the tissue paper, my name scrawled in familiar handwriting. I picked the note up, seeing a smaller box below it. Unfolding the note, I grabbed onto the counter for support as I read the words.

You asked me who I'd be if I gave it all up, and I couldn't answer you. But now I know the answer.
I'd be yours.

My chest seemed to leap to my throat, the wound in my heart so agonizing that I dropped the note. Slowly, I lifted the smaller box from the tissue paper and opened it, my breath catching as my eyes took in the diamond engagement ring that sat atop a receipt. I pushed the ring aside, my tears falling. The receipt was from a jeweler around the corner from his firm in Bridgeville. He had blacked out the price, but the date was visible—three days before Clint had attacked me. A small scribble was on the bottom, reading: *I hope this is her best Christmas ever.* More tears fell with the realization that Greyson had bought it, intending to propose on Christmas. The confirmation that he was telling the truth tore at me, twisting my thoughts and emotions about the situation and all he'd done.

I shoved the two notes in the box and put the lid back on. No longer hungry, I returned to my room and sat in my window seat, holding the box. I stayed there, dozing off and on through the night until morning lit my room. With it, no clarity came. Confusion was all that greeted me. How could I forgive him for what he'd done, no matter that he'd changed his mind? I opened the box again and took the ring out. The diamond was enormous, and it sparkled in the morning light.

There was a knock at my door, and I rolled my eyes. Mason had checked in on me when he'd returned, but I'd shooed him off, not wanting to talk to him about it. I was certain he knew what was in the box. He would have known it was from Greyson.

"Go away, Mason. I don't want to talk yet."

"Not even to me?" A mop of brown curls peeked around the door, her hazel eyes smiling at me. I hadn't seen her in years, but I'd have known the smile in those eyes anywhere.

"Casey?"

She nodded as she moved further into the room, and I put the box aside, jumping up to hug her. The appearance of my old friend could not have come at a better time. She was Tyson's younger sister and when their father died, their mother moved across the country to another province. Tyson had stayed with Mason, and I now understood why—they were in business together. Even though they were only twenty-one at the time, it had already started.

Casey had still been in middle school, so she'd had no choice but to go. She hadn't been back, and I'd missed her dreadfully, flying out to see her every so often with Tyson when he would visit her.

"I hear you're moping in here about a man," she teased, pulling a handful of my hair forward. "You look terrible, Ri. When was the last time you showered?"

I grimaced. It had been a few days, and I was sure I was ripe. I had no energy to even bother showering.

She glanced at the window seat before walking to the box and sitting. Her brown hair shimmered with highlights of red in the sunlight. I'd forgotten how pretty she was. She'd always been self-conscious of her fuller figure when we were younger, complaining that she wanted to be thin like me, but I didn't think she'd look as pretty if she were. She was beautiful the way she was, and I was happy she embraced it now and noticed how men watched her when she entered a room.

She peeked at me and patted the seat next to her as she fingered the ring. "This is some rock."

"Did you know?" I asked, sitting and pulling my feet to my chest.

"That a diamond this size existed?"

I pushed her leg with my foot. "No, smartass. About Mason and Tyson."

Her lips pursed, and she was quiet for a moment. "Yes. I knew when it first started. Tyson made me swear to keep it quiet because Mason didn't want you to know. It was one of the reasons my mom moved us and why I never returned. Tyson wanted me to stay far enough away so that nothing would happen to me." Her eyes searched mine. "I'm sorry, Ri. It wasn't my secret to share."

Laying my head back on the wall, I stared out at the snow, wondering just how naïve I'd been to live for so many years without seeing anything in my world for what it was.

"Do you love him?" she asked me.

It was a question I'd asked myself a million times, and the answer was always the same. "Yes."

"Tyson told me what happened. They would have killed him if he hadn't saved you. But they didn't, and I can tell you, that's saying something. Mason would take down anyone he thought was a threat to you."

"It doesn't matter. He used me."

"That's what Ty said, but he came here, Ri. You don't know what that means. Bosses don't step foot in each other's territories. Coming here risked his life and his entire organization, and let me tell you, Greyson Tides doesn't take risks that jeopardize his business." I gave her a questioning look. "I may be in another province, but that doesn't mean Ty hasn't trained me well. Mason made a mistake keeping you in the dark. You need knowledge to stay alive in this world, and he chose not to give it to you."

She handed me the ring. "He let you go, Ri. The guys know what that means. Do you?"

Standing, she kissed the top of my head. "I'll be here the next few days if you need me." She walked to the door, and glancing back at me, said, "Why didn't you tell me Mason was so sexy now?"

I gave her a grossed-out look.

"What? He is. Shit, those muscles and those tattoos."

"That's gross, Casey."

"Not for me," she said, giving me a wink before she closed the door.

I tried to clear the thought of my brother being sexy from my head. He was handsome, like my father had been, but sexy?

"Yuck," I mumbled.

Setting the ring aside, I rose, determined to shower and regain some sense of hygiene. Once I was clean, I forced myself to leave my room, leaving the ring behind. For the first time in too long, I spent the day with Mason, letting his smile at my appearance ease the pain in my heart. We shared dinner with Casey and Tyson, and I let Greyson slip from my mind for a few hours.

When the night ended, I returned to my room, my mind clearer. The ring was still on my window seat where I'd left it. I tried not to look at it as I prepared for bed, snuggling into a pair of snowflake pajamas Mason had gotten me for Christmas the year before. I sat on my bed, the diamond on the ring shimmering in the moonlight that poured through my window. I felt more like myself than I had in a long time, and with that knowledge came the realization that a part of me was missing. A part I'd given to Greyson. One I didn't want to take back. And that was what hurt so badly.

He'd let me go. Casey's words settled into my mind like a snowflake that nestled into your hair and refused to melt. He had let me go. If his intention had still been to use me, why push me behind him when Mason drove up? Why not hold his gun to my head like Clint had or kill me to hurt Mason? And why had he let me go? He and Mason were enemies. He could have easily taken me and shot them both before turning the gun on me. But he hadn't. He'd stood there, looking as defeated as I'd felt. Fractured. Just like I was.

I lay there, thinking through everything that had happened. The way I'd invited him in before I'd known he was my stranger. How he'd protected me from Matt and his lies and protected me from Clint. How he'd saved me and then let me walk away.

Pushing the blankets back, I went to my window seat and picked the ring up with the note.

Yours.

The word was a powerful one. He would be mine. He hadn't said I would be his like he had that day in his office. The day he'd claimed me. I wondered if he'd been playing his game then or if the game had changed for him.

He was giving himself to me, giving me his heart in that one word.

I slipped the ring on my finger, amazed at how he knew enough about me to know my ring size. He knew everything about me, yet I barely knew him. But I knew how he made me feel. The way he touched me, like he worshiped me. The way he made love to me. I knew the reaction he caused in my body and my heart. The way his grin could light me on fire, or his touch could melt me.

Lifting my eyes, I stared out at the silent landscape. I'd run two months earlier to escape a life I didn't want. Running right into that same life with a man who'd left his mark on my soul. Maybe it was time I stopped running.

I returned the ring to the box and rushed out of my room, finding Mason in the living room. His eyes were creased with worry as he held a glass of alcohol in his hand.

"Ri? Is everything all right?" he asked, the creases deepening.

"I want you to tell me all of it. Bring me in. Teach me. I want to know everything there is to know about this life."

The worry lifted, his smile returning. "Are you sure you're ready?"

"Yes."

"Then get your ass in the chair, Ri. Let's talk."

Spring had come, the bitter cold fading as the air warmed and the city returned to life. While I appreciated the winter, the rebirth of spring was usually a welcome sight. This year, however, it was only a reminder of how long it had been since I'd lost Riley. Each day that passed had not brought relief from the ache that was a constant companion. The pain that sat in my chest no matter how I tried to ignore it. Nothing gave me relief from it. I'd tried burying myself in my work. I avoided the street where her apartment had been. I tore my bedroom apart and redesigned it, erasing every trace of her, but nothing worked. No matter how I tried, I couldn't remove the mark she'd left on my heart.

I'd sent her the ring, having Sherry mail it out the next day. I lost what little hope I had when no reply came. No return note, nothing. And so I buried myself back in my work, watching as the snow melted the way Riley had melted my heart. Watching as the spring flowers poked through and wondering why my chest still ached, why an emptiness still existed that I couldn't seem to fill.

Folding the newspaper, I tucked it under my arm. The air was unusually warm today, and I'd left my coat at home. I made my way to the elevator, my eyes avoiding the firm's lobby like they did every time I walked by. I'd tasked Sherry with finding me a new office so I wouldn't have the reminders of Riley on the mornings I came in, but for now, I dealt with it.

I slid my keycard and pushed the penthouse button. As the doors closed, a heeled foot stopped them. I followed the line of the leg, recognizing the curves as my heart thudded. The doors closed, and Riley stood across from me. She was stunning. Her thick ebony hair was down, cascading in waves over her shoulders. She wore a tight black skirt that slit on the side and a loose silk shirt that sat softly on her chest, the buttons left undone just enough to show the swell of her breasts. Her emerald eyes were dark, nearly knocking me over with the confidence behind them.

She gave me a coy smile before hitting the emergency button, stopping our ascent.

"Miss Brinks," I said, hoping I was reading her right, but afraid of the pain it would bring if I weren't. "I thought I warned you about stepping into my elevator."

Her eyes twinkled with mischief. "Our elevator, Mr. Tides."

My breath caught, the strain of the past few months tempted to flee. She moved closer to me so that I could smell the light fragrance of her shampoo that mixed delicately with her perfume.

"Our elevator?" I asked, cocking my brow.

"Ours," she said, leaning into me. I dropped my paper and grabbed her waist, bringing her against me, that fear of misreading her still in the back of my mind and not allowing me to kiss her like I wanted. She searched my eyes, her fingers coming up to trace my face, and I closed my eyes to her touch. "If," she said, and I opened my eyes, caution returning to me, "you meet my conditions."

"Conditions? I don't do conditions, Miss Brinks."

"That's too bad." She drew from my hold, but I yanked her back to me. The feel of her body against mine brought me to life where nothing but death had seemed to sit within me since I'd lost her.

"But you might persuade me to make an exception," I said, moving my hand down to her hip. "Be a good girl and make me an offer."

Her lips parted, a tremble going through her body. The pain in my chest receded completely as my heart pounded in anticipation. I slipped my hand up the slit of her skirt, hitting the distinct feel of thigh highs attached to a garter. My dick jumped at the feel. I turned her so that I had her back pinned against the elevator wall.

"Conditions, Miss Brinks, before I lose my patience." Because I wanted to devour her, but I knew I needed to wait. Too much had happened between us, and I wouldn't risk losing her again.

"You bring me in. Make me part of the business."

I dropped my hands, stepping back. "No." The thought of her getting hurt again was too much. I still couldn't get the vision of her bloody and bruised face out of my mind.

Her jaw ticked. "Yes. You're not leaving me in the dark again. Neither you nor Mason. That's the reason Clint hurt me in the first place."

I bit back the rage at the mention of his name and replied, "It's too dangerous—"

"How could it get any more dangerous, Greyson? Clint almost killed me twice. It doesn't get more dangerous than that."

"Yes, it does. You could be dead," I said, hitting the elevator button. She pressed it again, and I shot her a look.

"You're not winning this. You don't get me unless I'm part of things. Mason let me on the inside, and I've spent the last month learning everything he could teach me."

I laughed. "Mason is a child in this business."

She leaned into me. "Then teach me what he couldn't."

I gritted my teeth, hating what she was asking because it

would expose her to everything she despised about me and the life I led.

"I can't love you completely if I don't know you, Greyson."

"What's the other condition?" I asked, hearing the bite to my tone.

"Who said there were only two?" she replied, knotting my stomach with worry about what could be next.

"What, Riley?"

"You return to working with Mason—"

"Fuck, no. I don't work with anyone." I tried to start the elevator again, but she stepped in my path. She was aggravating me with her conditions, none of which were ones I liked.

"Mason agreed to it, just like you offered when you agreed to find Clint. When you pretended you didn't know where I was and hunted the man who threatened to hurt me, agreeing to a truce with Mason to keep me safe."

"That was necessary."

"And so is this." Her voice held a plea I couldn't ignore. "Greyson, he's my brother. How can I be Mrs. Tides if my brother is your enemy?"

My jaw dropped, my heart slamming in my chest. "Mrs. Tides?"

She reached into her shirt and brought out the engagement ring, putting it in my hand. I let it sit there, staring at it, its weight increasing with every passing second.

I lifted my eyes to hers as she said, "If you want me to be yours, you need to meet my conditions."

Words failed to form as she held her fingers out toward me. "What's the last condition?" I finally asked, afraid to hear her answer. So far, her demands had been steep.

"That we have a Christmas wedding because I missed spending Christmas with you."

My smile was wide enough to cause my cheeks pain, the tightness in my chest burning with the love that hadn't faded.

"I think I can arrange that."

"And the other conditions?" she asked, as I took her hand.

"You're demanding, aren't you?"

"I can be when it's something I really want."

"And is this something you really want?" I asked, wanting to hear her say it. "To be my wife?"

"Are you asking me to marry you, Greyson?"

I slipped the ring on her finger, saying, "Yes. Marry me, Riley. Marry me, and I'll spend the rest of my life making up for the pain I caused, for the lies, for the—"

She stopped me with a kiss, throwing her arms around my neck, and I pulled her closer. I'd waited so long to hold her again, thinking I never would and tolerating the void that thought had caused in my chest. I never wanted to let her go again.

"I'm sorry, Riley," I said between kisses.

"I know." She pulled her lips from mine, her green eyes studying me. "Can we go home?"

"Home?" I asked.

"To our home so you can make love to me. I've missed your touch."

She reached for the elevator button again, and I stopped her. "I thought I told you there were consequences to walking onto my elevator, Miss Brinks."

She shivered deliciously.

"What sort of consequences, Mr. Tides?"

I gave her a mischievous smile and pinned her to the wall, relishing the hitch of her breath as my hand slid back up her skirt, skimming along her bare ass. Her eyes twinkled, and I cocked my brow.

"You said to leave the thong off next time," she said slyly.

"And so I did, Miss Brinks."

"Mrs. Tides," she corrected, making my heart leap to my throat.

"I'm going to ravage you in this elevator and mark it as ours,

Mrs. Tides." Saying the words left a tightness in my chest that reverberated through my body.

"Is that one of my consequences?"

"It's a start, but I stole some silk scarves when the movers packed your things that I might need to put to use."

The blush climbed in her cheeks gloriously.

"And a blindfold that fits perfectly over those gorgeous green eyes of yours."

Her lips parted, and I couldn't help but kiss her, letting the strain of the past few months slide from my muscles and the ache in my chest dissipate with each touch as I took her in our elevator. I spent the day making love to her, touching every part of her body that I'd missed and putting every sigh, every moan, every cry of my name to memory.

Riley was no longer running because I'd claimed her, and I would never let her go again.

About the Author

J. L. Jackola is a writer of love stories with fantasy, darkness, feisty women, and morally gray men. She's an admitted sugar addict with a penchant for anything with salted caramel. When she's not weaving tales, snacking on sweets, or downing her morning cup of tea, you can find her logging miles in her running shoes, watching movies with her family, or curled up with a book.

She resides in Delaware with her husband and three children.

To learn more, visit her website at
www.jljackola.com

www.ingramcontent.com/pod-product-compliance
Lightning Source LLC
Chambersburg PA
CBHW032249310726
48973CB00008B/2345